Messy

Katie Cooper

XOXO Hil St

Kaleb Muenoch

Brady Chen Lemore

FIRE

Copyright © 2016 Hilary Storm

First Edition

Cover Models: Dylan Horsch and Tessi Conquest

Cover Photography: Furiousfotog

Paperback Cover: Designs by Dana

Editing: Julia Goda

Printed in the United States of America

FIRE

By

Hilary Storm

&

Kathy Coopmans

PROLOGUE

KALEB

I can hear her in my ear as they pull away. The sound of her voice screaming keeps me fighting until I don't have a choice but to let them drag me from where I fell to my knees. There are too many of them. I can lie here and take their brutal attacks all fucking day, because I know she's safe. I'll play their games as long as it takes. I'll either die this way, or I'll kill a few of these motherfuckers and find my way out of here and back to her.

I feel the scrape of the gravel across my skin as my body is dragged to god knows where. My eyes are both swollen shut from some asshole's steel-toed boot to my face. I have no clue where I am; I only know there are tiny fucking pebbles digging into my flesh. My skin is on fire, and the reality of this hell begins to settle deep within my soul. *Fuck.*

These brutal fucks are about to eat me alive, and I know this is only the beginning of the torture I'm bound to receive.

I feel at least five sets of hands grip my body and throw me in the back of a truck like I'm a bag of trash. The landing only intensifies my already bruised ribs, but I welcome the pain. It means I'm still alive.

I focus on the noise around me, trying to memorize every single fucking sound. There's nothing but the harsh whispers of the night. I've been proficient in knowing every bit of my surroundings when a dangerous situation arrives, until now.

My focus shifts to the loud cawing scream coming from above. I can hear the vulture circling as if there's something here to feed off of. I refuse to believe that's my fate and silently will that fucker to choke on the next rotting flesh it preys on.

The rumble of the engine starting reminds me of the truck we were moved in earlier, but it's slightly smoother. I imagine an old farm truck with a similar bed as I'm flipped to my face, so some dickhead can tie me up tighter. The restraints are tight, and I'm trying my hardest not to fight back. I need the element of surprise on my side, and I'm positive having two eyes to see with will be a great start.

I focus on the movements of the truck as I'm being manhandled. The further away we get, the harder it is to swallow. I know it'll be hard as fuck for my team to search for me now. My only hope is to stay alive long enough for my guys to find me when they do return. They're the best at what they do, and they will find me. I'm just not sure how long it will take them. Their first priority is to get the target back to the States under any condition, and if any of them falter from that, I'll personally kick their asses myself.

The sound of the truck braking pulls me back to the reality of the nightmare I'm living. I'm lifted to my feet by the ropes I'm bound by and shoved face first off the back of the truck. My knees crack, and a sharp splinter of pain hurls up my leg when I hit the ground. I *will* kill these motherfuckers the second I'm free. I can smell their fucking filth everywhere and will never forget it.

The feeling of my body scraping against the ground again emphasizes the pain I'm trained to deal with. It doesn't make it any easier; in fact, knowing what is possible is far worse than being surprised about any torture coming my way. My body is fucking killing me, and I'm fighting the urge to vomit as they drag me into a wooded area. The rustling of dried leaves crunching under their boots on what I can imagine is a gravel road burns into my memory. I'm trying to focus on everything I can. Every single one of my senses is on high alert; it's vital I pay attention and focus on each one of them. I hope like fuck I'll need this information in the near future.

The voices speaking Spanish ring in my head long after I'm tossed into some sort of cold-cemented cell. The metal door is slammed, sealing me to my fate for now. These men have no idea who they have fucked with. I'll build my strength in here, if need be. My mind begins to run a race of its own. Time means everything in love and war. I refuse to believe my love ends here, so I use the memory of her to fuel me.

I roll over and spit out the blood that's pooling in my mouth and try not to think about anything but her. She's stolen my heart, and I know she has to be battling her own kind of internal war over the way the mission ended.

Jade's beautiful skin lights up my memories, and even through this fucking hell, I can feel her. I know she's mad as fuck and won't stop until she gets to me. This should be comforting to me, but it scares the fuck out of me. I can handle anything they do to torture me, but if they lay one fucking finger on her, it'll feel like I'm being gutted. It will absolutely devastate and destroy me.

I need to do everything I can to keep her in my mind, where it's safe. Whoever the hell is behind all of this can't know about her. She's my fucking weakness and my stone-cold strength. Right now, she's giving me the courage I need to get through this, no matter what my fate might be. I know my team won't let anything happen to her, so I just need to focus on getting myself out of here alive. That's all I can do for now. I'll let her be my angel in this hell, the woman I've fallen in love with, and she'll be the power behind my force and the reason I need to survive.

I hear more voices outside the door and work to translate their disgusting words that are barely audible to my ears. My knowledge of how this works should have me shitting myself in fear, but I'll be fucking damned if these assholes will ever smell fear coming from me.

I wish they'd come in here, untie me, and let me have a fair chance against their bullshit. Chicken shit motherfuckers. I know how this works. Most likely, I'll be left here to die unless they find a reason to keep me alive. In the grand scheme of things, that isn't likely. They can do whatever they want to me. I can spend the last few days of my life knowing I succeeded. I never once failed my country, and given the chance to do it all over again, I would in a heartbeat.

There's only one thing I'd do differently. I would have stayed away from her if I had known this was my fate. How was I supposed to do that though? She drew me in the instant I knew about her. I can't change it now, and even if I could, I'm not sure how I could have stayed away.

A tiny tear slips out of my eye and across my nose as I think about the way it should be. I was so close to having everything. My heart is still full, and even though I'll most likely never feel her soft skin again, I swear I can smell her right here and now. I swallow hard and acknowledge the reality of this situation. The odds of me making it through this are very slim. I can only hold on to the memories and die with a vision of her in my head.

Their voices get louder, and I translate a few of their words. They're coming in soon to attempt to get me to talk.

I will never talk. I swallow around the large lump in my throat and begin to accept my fate.

I'll die soon with only one regret. *Jade*

Chapter ONE

Jade

"Harris, let me go. I swear to God, I'll kill you." I pull out my pistol and set it right on his temple. He looks at me with a sadness that matches my own. I'm hurting so fucking deep I can hardly breathe, and I want nothing more than to kill someone. If I thought for a second it would bring Kaleb to me, I'd do it right fucking now. My hands are shaking. My finger rests on the trigger, while my eyes pierce through Harris'. *What the fuck am I doing?*

This isn't right. Nothing about any of this is right. We can't leave Maverick. Not after I fell in love with him. I'm pointing my gun at my best friend's head while my heart crumbles.

"Elliott. Stop. I'm on your fucking side. We're in this together, so put your damn gun down. The second we can separate from the team, we will. I'm going back to get him and so are you. You fucking know we have to get Al-Quaren back to the States, and we can't do that if we're acting on goddamn emotions. We did what we fucking had to do. Check yourself now, Jade. Right the hell now." He's right. I'm a mess, and yet here I am, still not able to put my gun down.

We both stand there in the same position as the thumping of the helicopter continues to move us. My head feels like it's about to explode and so does my heart. *How is this happening?*

I start to lower my gun, and he pulls me into his arms while the gun dangles in my hand. I'm dying inside, and the last thing I want to feel is the warmth of a man who is not Kaleb.

I slam the gun into my leg holster and push away from him, moving over to the monkey straps that bound me in earlier. I fight with everything I have not to kill every single one of these guys and try to fly this motherfucker back myself. *How could they lift off without him?*

"Ice. I'm working on a plan, and when we get to the drop, I'll take you myself." Jackson moves closer to me and talks loudly over the whipping of the helicopter blades.

That's three of us going. It sure doesn't feel like enough though, but with the rage I'm carrying, I don't care if there's an entire army waiting for us out there. I'll go in by myself if I have to.

"We have to play it safe, Ice. I can see crazy in your gorgeous eyes, and I can't let you go back in unless you reel that shit in. Do you fucking hear me? You're more of a danger to him and to all of us until you pull your goddamn shit together." Bullet is in my face, reminding me who's in charge here. The pounding of the helicopter blades literally matches my heartbeat, and I'm surprised I could hear his yelling over the noise in my head.

"Yes, Sir," I say loud enough for him to hear. Yet my tone is telling him I'm not really listening. I know what they're saying is vital and of the utmost importance, but I'm struggling like I've never struggled before.

I'm well-trained and knowledgeable about what can go wrong in a mission, but nowhere in all my life could I have ever prepared for the way I feel right now. They may as well have me, because I'm feeling every single fucking hit he's more than likely getting. I feel all of it. Straight to my heart.

"I'm killing the mics now. They have his helmet, and we don't need them listening in. We only have a few minutes when we drop. I want us all to board that airplane and regroup. It's the only way we know we're safe."

"Not on your fucking life, Kase." Harris comes in behind him and speaks before I have the chance to.

"Goddamnit. He'll have my ass if we don't do this right. We can't just start splitting up and fucking lose everyone. Seriously. Use your heads. Both of you."

"And you know time is of the essence in a situation like this. We have to split up. Half of us take this piece of shit in and the other half stay behind and blow off heads until we get Fire," Jackson speaks his mind. He seems to be pushing to stay behind, and for that I like this guy more by the second.

"You're fucking crazy if you think they haven't moved him. You're also an idiot if you go back there tonight. An army will be waiting to blow *your* fucking heads off." Kase is logical. I know he is, but right now, I don't want fucking logic. I want Kaleb back where he belongs. With me.

Kase continues to talk, and I try to hear him. But my mind is spinning with chaos, and my body is filled with so much hatred and adrenaline for those bastards that took him, I can't comprehend anything else.

"Who do we have here in Mexico we can trust?" Thank god for Harris right now. He's asking questions that line up with what I need to know. All my mind wants to do is betray me of the years of training I've had, while my heart screams louder than any drill sergeant ever has.

"The two men who helped us tonight, but you fucking know we made a lot of noise and we're not out of here yet. Who's to say the whole fucking Mexican Cartel doesn't know our allies by now. That's why we get in and get the fuck out. No questions." Kase looks at me as he talks. It's as if he's willing me to agree to leave Mexico and Kaleb behind. I shake my head. No way. I refuse. I will never leave him in this country. Not without me.

I feel the helicopter begin to slow just slightly. I knew the ride would be short, the drive over in the truck was as well. *Why does that seem so long ago?* I can feel panic begin to flow through my veins. My body is shaking, and I look at Harris while he yanks his helmet off and analyzes me. I see so much stress in his eyes as I watch them adjust to the fact I'm barely hanging on. He starts to speak to me calmly and with strength behind his voice.

"It's your call. I'm with you on this." He moves to me roughly and wobbly as the chopper works to land. I look down and try to comprehend what my mind is saying versus what my heart is screaming. "Elliott. I need you to fucking promise you won't do one damn thing without me. Don't get any fucking crazy ideas to run and try to save the fucking world by yourself. Do you hear me? I'm with you on this. Just say the motherfucking word." Harris touches my arm as he talks, and I try to comprehend what it is I want to do. I don't know what we're supposed to do. All I do know is, I have to go get him.

Kase pushes in next to Harris and starts to push his point even harder. "I have access to the best equipment in the fucking world. Not to mention insiders who can help. You two gringos will stick out like goddamn tourists, and not a person in this hell will give you information. We will go get him. I swear to you on my fucking life. But I refuse to tell him when I find him that I let his woman do some stupid bullshit, and now I can't even find her. Let me do what I do best. Then I fucking promise I'll let you help me blow these motherfuckers into an oblivion when I do locate him." He has no clue how much I want to believe what he's saying.

Is it wrong of me to want to go back there and try to save him now? I refuse to believe it is. I've let a man in. I've fallen in love and I can't give up on him this easily, no matter what it costs me.

"What if it's too late? What if he's dead? What if he's being tortured while we sit here and talk about what we can and can't do? Bullet, I'm a doer. I don't talk about shit, I do it. If you think I'm going back to the States so we can get around some goddamn table and map shit out, you're the fucking crazy one. Get on your shit here and figure this out. Find us a fucking hole to hide in and work from here. Because if you think I'll let you fly me thousands of miles away before I kill your ass, you'd better think again. I'm not leaving him. He'd never leave me." I point my finger at him. My eyes never once ceasing the deadly, truthful glare I give him. He stands fully once we hit solid ground, taking in my words. Harris stays lowered in front of me, and I look to him for what, I have no idea. For strength? For approval? For fucking guidance? I have no clue.

"I knew your ass had to be stubborn to land Fire." Jackson leans forward to get my attention.

"You nailed that shit on the head." Harris turns to add his input, and I ignore them all as I work to move from this confined space. I'm torn and deflated, but I'm so close to begging them all to go back with me.

"Alright, let's move." Steele turns his head around from the cockpit and yells at the team. I snap my head in the direction of Ace and Vice yanking Al-Quaren up by his restraints and pushing him to the doors. His slow energy pisses them off, and they start to walk him faster once their feet are on the ground. I'd like to shove my gun in his face and demand for him to talk, but I know damn well I can't. My hands are tied in every possible way.

Kase starts talking to the old man who's always helping while Harris never leaves my side.

"Elliott. What's the plan?"

"To find Kaleb," I say and continue to walk to god knows where.

"How do you plan to go about this?" He stops our progress by grasping a hold of my arm once we're barely inside the hangar. Harris spins me toward him, and I watch out of the corner of my eye as another pilot takes off in the helicopter, and the loud sound of the blades starts to move out of earshot as I think of my answer.

"Harris, I don't fucking know," I scream, trying to jerk myself free.

"We need these guys. Please tell me you see that." His eyes plead for a reality check from me. His grip is firm and yet somehow reassuring.

"I know." My thoughts are interrupted before I can continue. The airplane begins to move just as I see Kase and Jackson running toward us. The plane slowly rolls out of the hangar and into the night air. *They stayed.*

"Thank you," I whisper once they reach us. My hands haven't stopped shaking. Harris' hold on me is long gone, and Jackson nods while Kase ignores me. My temper drops, and now I can actually say my mind is aware of the actuality we are going to find him, so I listen.

"Alright, we need to get the fuck out of here. Ricardo here is going to move us southeast a ways. He has a small house we can hide in until we get our shit together." Kase won't look at me. You know what? I don't care. He damn well knows I'm right or he would have never stayed behind with us. And finally, I have a name to the man who we already owe so much to.

I follow them into an old, nasty van while Ricardo cranks the engine. "Thank you," I say sincerely. God, I could kiss him. He has guts. I'll give him that.

"My pleasure." He nods before he puts the vehicle in drive, and we ride for what feels like forever on the roughest roads I've ever seen. Potholes have my ass hurting with every jar of this piece of shit van. My grip is tight on the torn leather seat, and I'm barely able to contain my own strength as my knees knock together with all the bouncing. The cool material rips from my stronghold, and I feel exhaustion wash over me from everything that's happened the past few hours. *Someone buy this man a decent car, for god's sake.*

It doesn't take a genius to figure out this place is in a very isolated area. I had no idea Mexico had such an area full of trees. It's a damn forest out here, all secluded and dark. I'd be scared as hell if I was out here by myself.

The harsh sounds of the night do nothing to calm me as we move rapidly from the van into the tiny house. Ricardo speaks quietly to Kase at the door after he lets us in, his English broken but understandable. He only gets a few sentences out before he turns right back around and leaves us to the empty house.

Kase slams the door, and we all just look around the floor at the evidence of someone living here. From the looks of it, I imagine a very old woman. There are old, faded afghans as well as stained doilies draped over the rickety, wooden furniture. The place is small and clean, and I'm not complaining one bit about the shelter it provides us while we decide what our next move will be.

"He said there's a closet in the back bedroom on the right that has some sort of trap door. There's room for all of us and our shit back there. We keep it all there unless we're wearing it. If we hear anyone coming, we go in lockdown. He's going to help the others find us when they get back tomorrow. Until then, we work on a fucking plan of attack." His voice is angry, and I know he's irritated that I pushed to stay. *Maybe one day, he'll understand why I could never leave.*

CHAPTER TWO

KALEB

I try like hell to open my eyes with no luck. The vile smell of piss and stale cigarettes fills the air around me. At least that sense is still working, because I sure as hell can hardly see. And god, that smell is enough to make a dead man choke.

I'm thankful for the fucker who cut the rope off me before he shoved my face into the concrete floor. My wrists are fucking raw and my skin burns from the friction of the rope. Dried blood coats the welts left behind from them wrangling the hell out me.   Sliding across the floor to a corner, I try to pull together an ounce of hope in an otherwise hopeless situation.

I still can't see, so I begin blinking profusely, working to add moisture. *Fuck.* My eyes are so dry it feels like fucking sandpaper every time I move my eyelids. Hell, I know this is just the beginning of it. I can feel deep in the depth of my soul that this will be the worst shit I've ever dealt with. I just wish I could tell these fuckers to bring it. I'm ready, assholes. Try all you want, but you will never break me. You can't break something that's already broken.

I work to roll out the kinks in my neck from sleeping on the floor of this shitty cell. I'm still trying to pry my eyes open fully, but the dirt in the air and the dryness all around me do nothing to bring moisture to these bitches.

"Come on. Open. I fucking need you," I whisper, as if demanding my eyes to open will work. The more they open, the more I'm blinded by the scorching sun. My voice sounds like shit because I'm thirsty as fuck. I manage to work them into a sliver, and that's about all I can handle as I wait for them to adjust. My head nearly explodes from the sudden rush of light. *Shit.*

Every part of my body aches, but it doesn't stop me from standing. I want nothing more than to be prepared for what happens next. I need to know my surroundings, even if it's a fucking nine-by-nine goddamn cage. Knowledge is key in situations like this. That and patience.

My internal compass needs to know the direction they took me last night. I start to relive their every move as they tossed me into the back of a flatbed truck right after they stripped me bare of all my equipment, then tossed me around like a fucking rag doll. Fuckers stole my guns and every damn thing I owned except the clothes on my back. I hope like hell I have the honor to make them all pay for what they've done, because they can bet their asses I'm keeping score.

My eyes adjust even more as I move through the cage and work my way to the steel bars holding me here. My hands grip the bars tightly, and I imagine them slipping around the neck of whoever the hell is in charge here. Nothing would make me happier than squeezing the life out of any of the cock-sucking bastards who even think about keeping me locked here. They'll die if I'm given the slightest chance. The entire group of them will.

It's fucking hot and it's only mid-morning by the way the sun appears halfway in the clear, blue sky. I'm east of where we were. How far, I have no clue. Thank god for my inner compass keeping me somewhat informed, even if it's only giving me the slightest clues.

From what I can see, there isn't a damn thing around, except for a small house that looks like it could crumble to the ground at any minute. The dirty siding is hanging halfway off, and most of the windows are broken. The goddamn smell is enough to keep everything away from here. It literally smells like rotting shit. I've got to be on some rundown farm or an old plantation of some kind that's embedded deep in the woods by the looks and amount of trees off in the short distance. It's a real piece of shit place, telling me there won't be any visitors anytime soon, so my hope for an escape is diminishing.

I inhale once more, hoping to smell my Jade, but I only smell them. The stench in the air tells me they're close, and no matter how much I prepare for them, I know this is going to be the worst kind of hell.

Backing away from the heat, I begin to pace and think of a way out of here, but I have nothing. All I can think about is Jade. Her screams haunt me, and I can still feel her cries deep inside. Her threats for them not to leave me were serious, and I know she gave them hell like they've never thought possible. She is one stubborn woman, and that's just one of the many reasons why I fell for her.

There isn't a thing I don't love about her. If I'm lucky enough to get out of here, those will be the first words she hears from me. Then her sexy ass will be heaved up over my shoulder, and we will get away from everyone for a long time.

I run my hands down my face, thinking about the plans we were making. If only it really were that easy for us to be able to get away. We would have worked it out somehow, and now these piece of shit motherfuckers who stand in my way of freedom and happiness need to die.

My torn-up feet slap against the concrete as I move around without a single stitch of grace. They stole my boots. Either they wanted them, or they know damn well I'll try to escape the first chance I get. My guess is the latter. I'll give them credit for the only smart thing they could've done. They obviously have no idea who they've successfully kidnapped. They could strip me bare, and I would still do everything in my power to gut them and enjoy every fucking minute of it.

Jade. Fuck. I can't get her out of my mind, not that I want to. I want nothing more than to get back to her and my family. I just have to endure whatever these assholes have in store for me first.

Sweat starts to drip down my back and face. I move to sit back in the opposite corner away from the sun because I need my strength. Every. Last. Bit.

With my knees drawn up, I place my head against the wall and clench my hands in front of me. I work to think of my favorite times with her. As sick and morbid as it is, my cock becomes hard when I envision the last time I was inside her. The way she looked at me like I was her every damn thing. The way she finally gave in to her feelings and surrendered.

For the first time in my life, I have someone who I want nothing more than to share it with, to give her my all, and to hopefully someday watch her belly grow large with my child. I'd love to listen to her laugh right now. Hell, I'd love to fucking fight with her. Then we can make up. Shit, thinking about make-up sex has my dick twitching. She'd be feisty as fuck, trying to forgive me for whatever dumb shit I did, while I fuck her in the best way possible. I know I could shut her up. I have a way with her.

Oh, my Jade. She's so damn beautiful. I can feel her strength and determination sitting here. My head snaps up just as I think it. I open my eyes when I hear the word determination in my mind and think about the last words I heard her say.

She begged them to go back and not leave me. They better have strapped her ass down and made her leave with them. She can be a hellion, but I think the guys can handle her. Harris will protect her and I know my guys will too, especially Kase. He will for the very reason that I asked him to.

The thought of her being out here all alone sends a chill through my body. I know her. She'll stop at nothing to try to save me. They all will when it comes down to it. I know damn well it killed them to leave me behind, but they had to. I get it. Even though it would have broken me to leave one of them, I would have done the same thing. Get the target back to the States and then turn around and come for them with or without the help of the government.

She would've been the exception to that rule, and I'd be lying if I told myself any different. I'm afraid I would've taken us all straight back into hell just to get her.

*****

"Fuck," I mutter into this shithole. I must've drifted to sleep. The heat is so intense it's nearly suffocating me to death. If this is the way they think they can torture me, then they're idiots. I've survived in the desert and sweat my balls off for weeks on end. I've shit in places they've never dreamed of and even went days without food or water while the need to kill the enemy outweighed my thirst and starvation.

My eyes open wider now. Thank Christ. I know it's mid-afternoon without even having to stand up to look; the shadows casting on the opposite wall tell me.

It's then that I hear voices outside, growing closer. Their foreign words rattle off in my brain. I don't have a damn clue what they are saying. *Fucking pussies.*

Then I finally see them. They stare me down and I do the same. My will to survive glares back at them without any regrets. I feel like a hard, cold killer, and I can tell by the way they're looking at me they think they have me right where they want me.

I watch them and they watch me. They stand there in green army uniforms, talking like the trash they are. Assault rifles hang over their shoulders, and I begin to laugh in a very hideous voice.

"You can take that bottle of water you have in your hand and shove it straight up your ass, motherfucker," I say with my focus trained on the one with the bald head showing under his faded, red bandana he has tied into a fucking do-rag. His beard is unkempt, and I'd love to scalp it right off of his fucking face. His dark-black eyes are shooting bullets into my skull, and if looks could truly kill, I'd be dead on the spot.

It's time to make a move and piss these men off. If I piss them off enough, they'll make a mistake, and I just need one of them to fuck up for just one single second.

I stand tall with my shoulders squared back and my head held high, showing off the confident man I am. They have another thing coming if they think they can intimidate me. Hell, no.

My hands go to the zipper of my black cargo pants, while both of them watch in astonishment as I whip out my cock, take the two steps toward the bars to get to them, and piss all over their feet.

"Fuck you." My voice is deep, and stoic, and full of meaning.

The one I feel to be weak jumps back, cursing I assume, then walks away. Dick. While the idiot who continues to stare me down stands there until I finish and tuck myself back into my pants. He's probably some gay motherfucker that liked what he saw.

"You're brave." His speech is slurred and his accent is heavy as he takes a step toward me.

"You're dead." I'm glad to know he speaks English, even if he does a shitty job of it. It'll be better if he understands me.

"I'm not the one who's baking in the sun like a dead fish." He speaks with as much hatred for me as I have for him.

"Trust me. Once I shit down your throat and slice your head off, you'll be the one rotting like a dead fish," I talk through disgust and slowly emphasize on the word 'dead'.

This man and I battle over control even though he thinks I can't do shit while I'm caged in here. I only hope they make the mistake of assuming that. I'd love to prove to them that I'm the one who should be feared.

I'm a retired American soldier who has trained and worked his entire career to know what to do in a situation like this. I've specialized in this shit. I look forward to the moment they drop their guard and I get to show them just how experienced I am at this. They want me to get tired and let my guard down, but I won't. I'll pretend to, but I never will.

Let's play, motherfuckers. They may outnumber me and hell, may even get the privilege of torturing me, but these bastards will never fucking break me.

CHAPTER THREE

KALEB

"He warned us about you." He smiles, showing off his yellow teeth and proving his terrible hygiene while he stands in front of me like I'm supposed to know who the hell he's talking about. One thing is for sure; this fucker is taunting me. I'll play his game and be more than happy to show him what danger he's truly in. Besides, curiosity has me intrigued with who's in charge here. I'd love to know how the fuck they know who I am.

"Who, fuckface?" I stare him down, boldly demanding him to answer my question.

"You'll see." What a pussy. This man is about to die in less than sixty seconds. I've been waiting until he got close enough, but now it's time to move. While my eyes stay focused on his, I never move from the tiny, black dots of his bloodshot pools the whole time I devise my plan. My hands slither down the rusted bar, and he doesn't see it coming until it's too late.

The knife he had sheathed in his gun belt is now in my left hand, while I grip his throat with the other. Like I said, I'm experienced with this shit. It's too late for this man to try to sputter off shit in my language. He tries, but I tighten my grip and set the blade even closer to his neck.

"You scream, and I slice your fucking throat." He clears his throat the best he can, but the pressure I'm applying on his Adam's apple will have him dead in a matter of seconds. His eyes begin to bulge, while the knowledge of death begins to contort his face. He knows I'm killing him, and my heart begins to feel alive once again.

"Who the hell are you talking about?" I demand. This is his last chance to speak before he dies. The dire need to kill someone has taken over, and I'll be ready for the next one to come near my fucking cage.

"You'll see," he says once again. I snap then. This man is gone. Let him rot and stink up this fucking place even more than it already does.

While my hand squeezes more, his life quickly comes to an end. I lift the knife in the air while my mind loses control. I have it in me to slice and stab him over and over for having anything to do with locking me in this fucking cage. I've done it before and I will do it again after this one. I'll do whatever it takes to survive and get back to her.

His knees start to buckle, and urine covers his pale green pants. He needs to suffer more, and I watch in awe when the knife jabs into his tanned skin. My fingers lift one at a time as the knife glides across his throat. His blood oozes out and begins to bubble as its warmth mixes with this intense heat of the thick, heavy air.

I hold him upright while he chokes and gasps for his last bit of air. Blood coats my fingers and the color red spurs me on even more. I wish I was holding a gun in my hand to bring down every damn one of them out here, instead of this joke of a knife.

I scoff when I know he's dead. My arm is no longer strong enough to hold his dead weight through these bars, so I let him fall to the ground, hoping his soul is on its way straight to hell.

That's when I hear the voice of the man I haven't spoken to in years.

My fucking brother.

"Nice kill." Those are the words he says to me after not seeing him for years. The last time we spoke was when I hauled his ass out of a drug-infested home. He had a needle dangling out of his arm and puke all over his clothes. He was foaming at the mouth and not even coherent. For years, we tried to help him get his shit together.

I've shoved aside how I feel about losing my blood brother, but I will never forget the sobs, the prayers, and the way my mother blamed herself continuously for the way Ty lived his life. My mother lost her will to fight after the third time she convinced him to enter rehab, only for him to get out and jump right back in with the same crowd he ran around with. Dealers. Whores. Cold-blooded murderers. He's a pathetic disgrace to mankind, and now here he is, looking straight at my blood-covered hands.

"Walk closer, you crazy fuck. Let me do the same to you." I practically growl out my words through the hatred in my heart. I don't give a fuck if I carve his smug face up. The drugs have done a number on his sorry ass anyway. He's a few years younger than I am, but you sure as shit couldn't tell by looking at him. His once wrinkle-free skin is worn and crow's feet rest at the corners of his malice-filled eyes.

He's clean though and freshly shaved, which is more than I could say about him the last few times I saw him. His hair is slightly damp, and I can smell the soap from here. He smells as though he's just come from the shower. My own body itches to wash off this place's disgusting odor.

"Drop the motherfucking knife, Kaleb, or I'll shoot you with your own fucking gun." He whisks my pistol out of the back of his pants. The silver metal of the barrel shines daringly in the heat of the sun as I watch his cocky-ass smile on his face. He's loving this.

I weigh out my options, which are fucking slim. I know he'd love to shoot me and would probably announce to the world he's the one who had the honor.

I drop the knife, and the loud clank of the small blade echoes in the tiny cell as it crashes to the cement floor. I'm not giving up. I'm playing his game. I want my hands on this fucker. He knows it too by the way he walks toward me. He's scared, as he should be. That's why he has me caged up.

"How are mom and Amelie these days?" he asks with not a damn ounce of sincerity in his tone. I say nothing. Instead, I cross my arms over my chest. I'm done talking. No way will I feed into his shit, nor will I have a friendly long-time-no-see conversation with him.

"I don't have time for you to answer me anyway. I'm about to fuck up your life, Kaleb. Mom's little golden boy. How does it feel to know that perfect fucking life you live is about to be over?" I seethe inside as I listen to his confidence. "Mom considers me dead. Well, it's about time to show her what dead really looks like." He stops walking to speak directly in front of me. "I wonder what she'll think when she opens the box with your fucking head in it." His eyes stare into mine, and I want to fucking rip them out of his face and force them down his throat. He knows our mother is a sore spot with me, and I know he'll use her to try to get through to me. *Thank fuck he doesn't know about Jade.*

He watches me as he dials a number on his phone.

"Get someone down here and bury Raphael. His weak ass is dead thanks to my brother. Preferably Chico, since he was sent down here and obviously took off like a motherfucking chicken. Then, when he's done digging the grave, shoot him and bury them both." He snaps his cheap burner phone shut. He keeps the gun trained on me as he bends down and grabs the dead man by his hair. His unfocused, dead eyes are wide open and staring off into space as he drags him off to the side.

"Now, time for some fun. Since you seem to be some badass military expert, shackle yourself." He drops a duffle bag down and pulls out a set of shackles. He throws them on the ground in front of the cell and stares at me to move.

"Do it, Kaleb, or I swear I'll shoot you then cut your pretty boy head from your body. I'm itching to cut that fucking mom tattoo off your skin and ship them both to her." I'd be a fool to admit that every time he says 'mom' I cringe inside. There's something in the way he looks at me. His gaze is void of any emotion or sign that we have the same blood running through our veins at all.

I do as I'm told, but I take my time. He steps in closer when I'm bent down, cuffing my legs together. He steps on the knife and slides it out of my reach. *Smart man.*

Still saying nothing, I lift up and the chains hang free. I clamp one against one wrist then shrug. *Fuck him.* He can do the other. Ty tucks my gun in the front of his pants, leans in with sturdy hands, and locks it in place, then steps back as we both turn our heads to the sound of men approaching.

Their Spanish words throw chaos into an otherwise silent room. They converse back and forth with my brother. His mouth moves and his nostrils flare. Then out of nowhere, he backhands the asshole that was here earlier with the butt of my gun. The gun busts open his cheek, and blood instantly drips over his mouth.

My brother surprises me with his raw violence. His actions are ruthless, which proves he's so far gone from reality there's no getting through to him. I'm positive about one thing, I want my damn gun back. If I make it out of here alive, that's the weapon my brother is going to die from as I take my last step from this fucking filthy shithole.

"Get him out of there. Wrap this around him first."

"You afraid to do it yourself?" My silence wavers.

"Nah, man. If these assholes want to be fed and keep fucking their wives, then they do as they're told. Otherwise, they die. Then I'll fuck their wives. Isn't that what a good leader does, brother? They give orders, and their servants do what they say?" The slimy bastard is trying to push my buttons and make me angry. His provoking won't work.

"Nah, man. That's not how it goes at all. You see, in my army, in my country, we kill the enemy, not our brothers." I'm not even going to respond to his comment about what he might do to women. That will fester inside of me until I rip him apart. His brows quirk up. I know damn well he understands my meaning when he blinks several times. His throat bobs up and down as he contemplates his next sentence to me. He may be my blood brother, but the men I serve with know what it's like to be a real fucking brother.

"You think they'll come back for you, don't you? They may, but they'll never find you. I'm going to torture you, Kaleb. In ways you've never heard of, never seen, and never even knew existed." Ty is so full of hatred as he begins to bark out his disgust for me.

"Strip his clothes off," my brother demands one of his coward followers to come near me after he unlocks the small door. I'm escorted out of the cell with my own gun aimed right at me.

The light is blinding to my sensitive eyes. The butt of a gun is shoved into my back as we walk several yards. We stumble toward a tree with a rope hanging down from a sturdy branch. *Awe, shit.*

He's going to leave me out here, baking in the sun, after he fucks me up. *Fuck.*

His stupid subjects cut my damn clothes right off of my body, the knives digging into my skin as they do, and I continue to keep score. I can feel the blood slowly trailing down my arms and legs. *Goddamn, these fuckers are going to pay.*

A knife lies at the base of my throat while they unhook the cuffs from my arms. Determination courses through my veins as I look for my out. I could kill one or two of these fuckers before my brother shoots me, but I'm better off letting him bring his torture on while praying like a bitch my team is on their way back here by now. I know their training will lead them to me.

I'm standing naked in front of these bastards. My legs are still bound together by the chains as they draw my arms up tight with the rope. I will my dick to fucking tuck itself into my body and pray they don't do what I would do if the roles were reversed right now. *Fuck.*

"I was one happy motherfucker when I got the call they had you. My piece-of-shit brother sniffing around in my world." He moves in closer to my face, spitting each word at me. Come closer, asshole. Come an inch fucking closer. There's a little army here to watch the show, but he's the only one I need to focus on.

"If I gave you one call, would it be to our sweet mother? Would you call to tell her that her piece-of-shit son has you bound to a tree with your dick hanging there, lifeless, knowing your fate? Or would you call that sexy little Sniper you had with you?" My gut twists as he probes for the tiniest clue that she's a weakness. I will never show emotion when he talks about her. Thank fuck I'm experienced with this shit. I remain quiet and wait for what he has next. He may think he knows what the hell he's doing, but he'll make a mistake. And by god, when he does, I'll make my move.

"Where did they take him?" He starts to pace in front of me, and I stay stone-cold. He'll never get me to talk, and he knows this.

One of the guys hands him a whip, and I take a deep breath right before the leather lands across my upper thighs, missing my dick by about an inch. *Fucking hell.* Let it begin. I swallow the pain and hold my breath, while I prepare my mind for more torture.

"I'm not going to ask you again after this. You'll get one question a day. You'll eventually talk, or you'll hang here, withering away until you die."

"Where did you fucking take him?" I prepare myself for the next blow, but fail. My eyes slam closed as the pain rushes through my body and the feeling of my skin ripping open pierces through me. This time, he didn't miss. The tip of the whip cracked right across the head of my dick.

I've drawn my legs up with the natural instinct to protect myself, causing my arms to pull tight with the weight of my body. My skin begins to stretch, and pain spreads over me entirely. I eventually lower my legs again to stop the stretching, but the urge to vomit still fills me.

"The strong brother. Looks like a fucking pussy to me." He cracks the whip again, fucking hitting me in the same spot, and I can't stop from bending into the fetal position again. Drawing my legs up as I try to comprehend the insanity going through my mind opens me up to even more torture. My eyes pinch tight, and I'm barely breathing through this nightmare.

I hear another crack in the air behind me and feel the bottoms of my feet burn from the contact. Again. And again. And again.

They continue until I finally straighten my legs below me.

I'm burning. My skin wants to crawl away from the abuse, but I'm stuck here. Hold your shit together, Fire.

"Are we going to do this all fucking day? Because I have to tell you…. I'm enjoying this shit." Bile rises to my throat when I speak, and I crave the kill of him like I've never craved anything before. I want him dead. He's not worth the air he breathes, yet my life is in his hands right now.

"You know, it's been ten years. Ten fucking years since you turned your back on me. I should thank you." His obscene laughter fills my ears as I wait for him to continue.

"It was because of you that I found my home here. Who knew Mexico would welcome a piece of trash like me? Who knew I'd get to work with the world's finest? And who fucking knew… I'd have the opportunity to revisit my old demons here today?"

I can feel blood seeping from my feet as I slowly adjust my legs until I feel the dirt below me. He says all I have to do is give up Al-Quaren's location, but I know that's signing my death papers. I can't do that. For one thing, the team won't take him to the same location. It's something I'd do too if I were in their situation, change the plan. Ty needs this man for something. I'm just not sure what.

"Why do you fucking care where he is?" I speak through the dryness in my mouth and watch the anger rise in him even more.

"Because there's a fucking price tag on my goddamn head for letting him get captured under my watch." Ah, I get it now. He fucked up and now he's scrambling. In some fucked-up way, this brings joy to me even in my current state.

"Do you remember burning me?" Ty steps right up to my face. Damn. He's quick to change the subject.

"Nope," I say.

"Of course, you don't. I'm going to have fun reminding you of all the bullshit you did to me growing up." I watch a man come from the house with a large pot of something steaming. I know shit is about to get really bad, and all I can think about is him getting just a little fucking closer.

He nods as the man gets near me, and in the next second, my skin erupts as hot water burns nearly every inch of the front half of my body. Oh my god. The fucking pain.

Ty steps right up to my face, clicking his tongue as he takes a stroll down memory lane. I remember burning him, alright. The two of us tried to make mom some coffee. I accidently spilled the entire pot down his front. He squealed in pain and I cried. God, we were so young, and I felt terrible for it. But this, the pain he is inflicting on me now, makes that small pot of coffee nonexistent. Our mother took care of him. He was rushed to the hospital, and his burns were cared for immediately. He came out unscathed.

His laughter erupts, and I listen to gunfire going off before the sounds of them walking away calm my mind in the slightest way. I'm left hanging from this half dead tree with my scorched body becoming hotter by the second. I work hard to keep my mind focused on my blond-haired woman. *Jade.*

CHAPTER FOUR

KALEB

My skin is fucking raw. One minute, my chest feels like a burning fire that simply won't calm down, and the next, I can't feel a thing. My internal emergency system is shutting down and the pain-killing chemicals are steaming through my veins, causing my blood to boil from anger. My own brother is behind the torture, and his hysterical laughter after each session tells me he's enjoying it immensely. It's a different feeling when the enemy is my own flesh and blood.

I've been beaten with a whip among many other things. The first striking sensation brings fire to my skin, then every strike, slash, and gouge after pulls a numbness to the surface that nearly matches my internal feelings about everything in the world, except my hatred for my brother and my love for Jade. A slow burn continues down my back as my skin continues to be ripped apart, and the feeling of blood dripping after a few strikes reminds me I still actually have feeling in some places.

And my dick. That motherfucker will pay for that one. I've never felt pain like a straight-up strike from a leather whip can cause to my dick before in my life. You could shoot me. Stab me. Burn me. But this...I have no fucking words. Not a damn thing to explain the pain that continues to shoot through my balls, up my spine, and through every other muscle in my body. It's a constant suffering that's indescribable.

The minute my body tries to relax is the minute the excruciating shit zig-zags throughout my entire nervous system. I physically want to shut down and drop my dead weight right here, but I won't. Revenge is a beautiful thing, they say. I'll get mine. On every last one of these drug-smuggling heathen motherfuckers.

Now, my skin itches, my muscles cramp, and my arms shake from the uncontrollable urge to writhe their way out of these restraints.

He will not break me. The drug king piece of shit.

"Motherfucker," I whisper into the night.

Jade. My mind needs her. My body is beaten down, and I'm so damn weak and tired. My will to live for us will endure the physical pain they inflict on me. It's my damn heart that's breaking and splitting in two. For her. All for her.

I throw my head back, wincing as my skin pulls tight on my chest. This is all kinds of fucked up. I desperately try to vision Jade standing in front of me, but somehow I can't. All I can see is the loathing on my little brother's face. All I can hear is his laugh when the whip cracks against my skin and his hateful words of how I ruined his life as they echo through the night air.

I'd be a liar if I said I'm not hurt. My heart is bleeding out as bad as the cuts on my skin. Worse even. This is my kid brother.

The memories flood my mind about the trouble we used to get into. Boys being boys. Teasing our sister. Threatening her boyfriends. All of it. That is, until he fucked up his own life, by his choice. Sticking a damn needle in his arm and coming home like he thought I was going to pat him on the back for flying so high he couldn't see straight.

"You ruined your own life. Not me."

"Is that so?" His deep, slurry voice calls out from in front of me. I snap. My vocal chords strain and fight against me to speak to a man I don't even know anymore.

"Damn right, it is. You decided to fuck up your life, not me. And now, look at you. You're worn. Your skin looks like shit. You disgust me, little brother." Hissing through the agony of my battered body and my broken heart, I fight to leave him with words that will haunt him during his deepest, darkest nights. He'll remember this until he dies, we both will. Now is my chance to give him this little going-away talk. Because I'm

afraid that one way or another, I'll be going away from this
soon.

"I'm not the one hanging by a tree with my bare ass and
my worthless dick dangling in the breeze. It isn't my raw flesh
waiting for one of these vultures to swarm around here and pick
at my fucking bleeding skin. So, you tell me who looks like shit,
smells like shit, and is about to eat fucking shit if he doesn't shut
his fucking mouth." He grinds his cigarette into the ground
before he takes a swig of whatever he has in his bottle then
stumbles his way to an inch within my face. His breath is
disgusting, and his eyes flare with a loathing desire to just end
me. His nostrils move in and out like the madman he is while he
shows an ounce of restraint in his actlons.

"You high, drunk, or both?" I question. Not that I give a
rat's ass, but my intelligence needs to know what I'm up against
here. If he's drunk, like I suspect he is, a nice head butt to the
face should knock his stupid ass out and break his nose. Fuck. I
wish my legs were free. I'd bash his skull into the ground once
he drops, then I'd make damn sure they wouldn't be able to
identify him. No one would miss him anyway. He's been dead
to us since the day he disappeared. Well, dead to everyone
except our mother. Yet, he has no remorse for what he has
done to her. I'll let the runaway continue to think she hates

him, because there's no way in hell I want him to think he has an in with her again.

Part of my brain tells me I no longer have a brother and that I hate this individual in front of me for the pain he has caused not only today, but to my family for years. I'm preparing myself for another physical attack, while he staggers toward me. Another part of my brain continues to analyze and count down to the second until I'll move to strike against the man I despise.

"I'm not on drugs anymore. Haven't touched them in years. Not since I learned you can make a hell of a lot more money selling than shooting up. I'm a rich bastard, Kaleb. This piece of shit place you see here is a front to the mansion, the pussy, the money, any damn thing I want. It's all behind you. Tucked nice and safe in the middle of this jungle." His hands go out wide, like he's the king. Maybe he is down here, but he's a motherfucking peasant to me. An absolute nobody.

He lifts the bottle to his lips and tips it back before he wipes them with the back of his hand.

"Let me check out my work." Stepping around me, he kicks at my legs. I fight like crazy to keep them from buckling. I'm afraid if they do, my arms will break and my shoulders will dislodge from their tight joints. His slimy fingers run across my sore skin like he's admiring a canvas he's painted.

I close my eyes, fading away inside, when he pours the alcohol over my ripe skin. *Goddamn shit, fucking hell, that hurts.* My eyes are closed tight as I dig deep, holding my breath, waiting for the pain to subside. It may sting like holy hell right now, but fuck me, he did me one hell of a favor by killing the infection and the bacteria I know damn well was building on my back. I need him in front of me. Face to face. There isn't a damn thing I can do when he's behind me. The only weapon I have is my head and the first chance I get, I'm using it.

"If you expect me to bow, then you may as well kill me now. I couldn't care less how much money you have, or anything else for that matter. You can kiss my bare ass while you're back there. However, you pansy ass, what I do care about is how in the hell you and I have the same mom. A woman who would have laid her life down to protect you. A woman who worked her fingers to the bone and did everything right by you, and yet you still broke her heart. That's all I want to know. Everything else you can shove up your selfish little ass. No, wait, before you shove anything up your ass, I understand why you took off. You're just like our father. A piss-poor excuse of a man. A deadbeat. A goddamn loser." I become furious at the same time I'm relieved he's finally right where I want him. I spit in his face just to get him even closer. I'm baiting him, and he's taking it just like I want him to. Before he gets a chance to answer me, in fact the very second he steps in front of me, I smash my forehead into his face.

The bottle clanks to the ground. His arms and shoulders automatically lurch forward. His body moves backwards, while his head snaps back in a whiplash motion.

He's knocked out in one fucking blow.

And I'm still standing. With my fucking arms tied to the damn tree.

CHAPTER FIVE

JADE

"What's taking them so long?"

"Jade, it's only been ten hours. They'll be here as soon as they can." Harris' tone is calm, while I'm anything but. My arms are craving the man I desperately miss. I just feel the need to hold him. I ache to soothe him from the torture I know he's endured. He needs to know how much he means to me.

"We should be doing something. How can I just sit here, knowing they have him? I have to do something, Harris." My pacing is out of control, and my mind will not stop with the nightmares that could very well be Kaleb's reality. I'm scared to death I'll never see him again.

"Okay, fine. You need a distraction. Tell me how the two of you got to where you are now. How did a man get so deep into your heart so damn fast?" I stop walking, not sure how to take his question. Is he being accusatory? Or just genuinely curious? Looking at his face, I quickly see he's being sincere and worried about me. I let the past few weeks rush over me and play through my mind, trying to determine the exact moment Kaleb Maverick made it through my wall.

"I don't know what it is about him, Harris. He just hit me hard from the first fucking moment I saw him."

"You do realize where you were when you first saw him?" Of course, I do. How can anyone forget?

"Yes." I continue looking at him, not sure where he is going with this either. He stands and moves closer to me, his arms going around me when he gets close enough. I embrace him, because right now, I need to pull from his strength. I'm holding back the tears that are beginning to fall. I need to remain strong in all of this, but I'm on the verge of falling apart. One slip of my mind, and I won't be able to function. I won't be any good to anyone, and right now, Kaleb needs me. I need to stay focused.

"As good as we would've been, I'm glad he stopped us." His deep voice continues just over my shoulder as he pulls me into a tight embrace.

"You and me both. I mean, can you even imagine?" He takes a deep breath, exhaling slowly.

"No." He holds me a few seconds longer and then steps away. "So this man hooked your ass, then you left him in Mexico?"

"Okay, jackass. You made me leave him in Mexico. I wanted to go after him." My voice gets louder than I plan, and I'm sure the others can hear me getting riled up again.

"Jade. Please tell me you can see how terrible of an idea that was? Tell me you know we had to fucking move and we nearly waited too long as it was."

"I know." I don't want to admit that I fucking get it, but I do.

"Would you really have shot me in the damn temple?"

"Do you really want me to answer?" Honestly, I don't know myself, but in that moment, I had it in me. All I remember is the anger flowing through my veins the further away I got from Kaleb.

"I know the answer." He sits on the tiny bed covered with a ragged quilt. I'm trying like hell to calm my insides so I can think straight, but I can't seem to feel any relief.

"Please, don't take it personally. I hated leaving him with everything inside me. I wouldn't have wanted to leave you either. At the time, I wasn't thinking clearly. You have to know I wouldn't have been able to pull that trigger. However, I have a loyalty to all of my brothers, and I don't falter, it's just hard to differentiate that when there's a higher mission involved."

"I know you do. I get it. I would've been insane if it had been you on the ground." I watch for his meaning behind it, wondering where all of this is coming from. I have to ask.

"You do realize there will never be anything between us?" His shocked look tells me more than the words he follows with.

"Shit, I know. Jade. You'll always be a sister to me, and I'd do anything for you, but you'd drive me fucking crazy. But that doesn't mean I'll let anything happen to you or let you get into a situation like going up against a Mexican army to save the fucking day." He stands again, crossing his arms to lean against the door while he continues. "I'm not asking all of this with any personal intentions. I just want to hear how the big, bad Jade was conquered." Under any other circumstances, I might find this conversation funny.

"I don't know. He just got to me," I leave him with the simplest answer, knowing I have no idea myself. "He consumed me, and now I feel fucking lost." No one knows when the right person is going to walk into their life. When they're going to consume their every thought. One day, I was walking around alone, then the next, he was all I could think about.

The room is quiet for a few minutes, and we both remain completely frozen in our positions.

"I promise you, I'll be with you until we find him." This is why I love Harris. He's loyal. We've been through shit, and he's still ready to lay it all down for me. He's my ride-or-die guy, and I'm happy as hell to have him here with me. Even though I threatened to kill him.

"I appreciate that. You know if we don't find him... Or if..." I can't finish that sentence. Harris is at my side when he realizes I'm struggling.

"That's not an option. We will find him. We will bring his giant, stubborn ass back to the States, and we can go back to my ranch. I will personally pay for a room in town, so you don't scare my horses next time." His laughter makes me feel slightly better, not that I can really feel great in this predicament, but I'll take an ounce of relief from the stress. Crap, I'll take anything right now.

I hear an engine getting close to the house, and we both throw our guards up quickly. Kase opens the door without warning and barrels into the room with Jackson on his heels. "Get in the hole now." My heart slams into my chest as we begin to rush into the perfect standing concrete casket big enough for about five people. They've all pinned me to the back wall like they have to protect me. Idiots. If they only knew I could shoot a bullet through all of their heads and still hit my target. It doesn't matter; every one of us has our pistols drawn while we wait for any sign of life outside this hole.

The engine dulls out just before a few car doors slam shut. I draw in a breath, preparing to shoot anything that opens that door. How I wish it were the men who have Kaleb, so they would beg me for mercy before I cut their balls off and shove them up their asses for taking him.

"It's me." We hear Ricardo from the other side of the door. "And us." My eyes grow wide. The rest of the team came back.

"Took you fuckers long enough," Jackson bellows out the door first, his big-ass frame hardly squeezing through the door.

"Fuck off, Jackson, who will get no action." Steele laughs at his own joke. While I just want to jump in everyone's arms and thank them for coming back, but I won't.

"You still pissed off at us?" Ace—or is it Vice? —slings his arm around me, tugging me close to his side. My mind is such a cluster I don't remember who is who anymore.

"No. You did what you had to do. I'm glad you're all here now. I'm assuming the mission is accomplished," I say bitterly. Not at them, but if it weren't for the man we had to go in and get, the man I care about would not be wherever he is, more than likely accepting the idea of death over his suffering right now.

"Yes. He's been handed over to the higher ups and... before you ask. They've been interrogating him, but he won't give up a damn thing. We're on our own from here, unless we get word from the President or his cabinet." He grins down at me as if I don't understand how this all works. I do. I know more than he thinks I know. What I want to know now, though, is what I'm about to ask our friend here. He sure has his way of getting around without telling us a thing. I'm just about ready to go off on the old man when Harris cuts me off. The look in his eyes tells me to let it go.

"Did you find out anything?" Harris directs his attention from me to Ricardo, even though he never takes his eyes off of mine. I blow out a heavy breath in frustration and work to focus on Ricardo's response.

"I haven't. They've vanished. However," he holds his hand up and signals for us all to follow. Harris and I drop our gazes from one another. I'll keep my mouth shut for now and let his logic lead this conversation over my emotions.

"There are a lot of wooded areas around these parts. Lots of vacant, run-down homes. Now, look." Pulling a map out of his back pocket, he folds it open on the table we all gather around.

"Harris," I say nervously. It's all in Spanish. I can't make out a thing.

"I got it, Jade." Harris nods then follows the old man's pointed finger as he places it on a spot on the map.

"Right here. This... this is where they have to have him." My anger propels. I'm speaking my mind this time.

"You can't just guess. You have to be sure. This isn't hide and seek. That's my man out there." Motioning to the door, I stop as I realize my voice is much louder than it should be. My emotions have me spun so tight I can hardly think straight.

"What she's trying to say is... We need some sort of verification before we go in and raid these places. Can we trust someone to go in and check some of them out? Maybe a local who won't look as obvious as this team," Harris explains.

"I'm not guessing. My sons have been out there. I'm telling you, this is where he is." He jabs his finger into the exact same spot on the map. I should feel like a bitch for doubting his word after everything he's done for us, but I don't. Our safety is vital during this. If I succeed at rescuing Kaleb only to lose some of his men, I'd never be able to live with myself.

"How can you be sure?" Kase stands tall beside this little old man who has gone out of his way to help us.

"Because there is a man hanging from a tree." I may still be standing, but my mind is now perfectly clear. I need to kill someone right the fuck now. Blood rages through my body, and I can't stand still another second. It's time to go in.

CHAPTER SIX

JADE

I'm crouched down alongside Harris. He demanded I not leave his side the second we piled out of the back of the truck. We have enough ammunition to blow up everything in this wooded area. I'm not about to ask where it came from. In this particular situation, I couldn't care less if the shit is stolen or if it belongs to the president of Mexico or the damn Queen of England herself, as long as we get Kaleb. Kase forced us all to implant a GPS tracking device into our inner leg, just in case one of us gets captured. I love that he has the technology and the initiative to get us this in such a short time. I could see Kaleb loving this idea.

The giant bushes and trees make it hard to see. The thicket is grouped together like the overgrown tangled mess it is. This shit needs to be bulldozed down, but I'm sure they consider this a form of protection for their shitty structures hidden behind it. How sweet it would be to drive up through the darkness, mangling these half dead tresses of trees in an Abrams tank. Then blow these fuckers up who dared to take Kaleb. My fingers start twitching; the stress I've been under is becoming an addiction, a devotee to my life for the past few weeks, and I want it gone. It may never leave my side. Hell, I may be on medication for the rest of my life, especially if things work out between Kaleb and I.

That single, one-syllable word ricochets throughout my body like I hope one of my bullets does soon through Kaleb's captors. I shouldn't be thinking about anything else right now, except the plan we have to get him out of there. I know he's here. I feel him. My need to be close to him and save him is blinding me right now. I've been as strong as I could be throughout all of this, and now when I should be resilient to anything... that's when the tears threaten to fall.

"You hanging in there, Elliott?" Harris whispers, nudging my side.

"I'm good. I want this done." I even try to sound confident. Both of us know good and well I'm far from it right now. Hell, in the time we've known each other, I've always been the most confident bitch alive, but today...Today is different.

"Fuck. Someone's flipped on a light in the house," Harris says with hope. God, let whomever the hell it is take us right to Kaleb. I find myself grinning, now hoping I'll get the opportunity to kill because I'm craving it.

"We need to wait for the go-ahead from Kase, Jade." Does he think I'm an idiot? I know that. Just because I'm antsy doesn't mean I'm going to shoot bullets into the thick goddamn air.

"Where the hell are they? They should all be here by now." Harris, Jackson, Steele, and I took off through the woods. While Jackson and Steele kept going deeper to guard and get into position on the other side of the house, the two of us stopped here. This is taking too damn long. The thought of it being Kaleb hanging there has tears once again stinging my eyes. My heart is barely beating; its own repair depends on what we find when the moment strikes for us to move in. Hurry the hell up. Someone make a damn move.

I adjust my scope when I finally see movement inside the house. This place is a fucking dump. The poor, barely-there structure would be better off burned to the ground.

Lights flicker on outside just before two men walk out in soldier's uniforms. I wince when I see one of them with the American flag stitched on the upper side of his arm. I damn near combust internally. If there is one single American who has anything to do with this at all, they will pray to the god above that they were born anywhere except the United States by the time I'm done with them.

"Motherfucker," Harris hisses. His voice is pained with the realization of what's happening.

"What?" I'm instantly horrified by his response. I aim my scope and watch their every move as they lead me right to my worst nightmare.

"No." I shake my head. My entire body goes into tremors when I see the lonely figure hanging from a large limb of a tree just like Ricardo said.

"What the hell have they done to him?" Harris continues to whisper in a voice filled with a similar hatred to my own.

It's Kaleb. I know it. His head is hung low and his arms are pulled tight by a rope above his head. This is the first time looking through my scope that I wish I wasn't seeing the sight before me. The night they took him comes rushing back to me. Even though I barely understood the words they were saying, there was no way to misread the anger and hatred they had for Kaleb. We left him to this fate. I will never forgive myself for this.

They have beaten the hell out of him. He's naked. The man I love is fucking naked and hanging from a tree.

The sight before me makes me sick. Yes, for the exact reason that it's the man I love. He's the man I'm here to bring home with me and so very far away from this shit I'm seeing today.

"Harris. Please tell me he's breathing. I'm sorry. I'm losing it here," I whisper the truth. I'm fucking losing it. Everything I've learned ceases to exist right now. I need to know. And yet, I can't look. Seeing him like this is ripping my heart out. This marks the second time in my short-lived life that I've had my heart traumatized. I can't breathe. The first was when my brother died, and now this. Seeing a man so strong hanging there, lifeless, all bloodied and abused. *How could they do this?*

I focus on pulling my shit together. Then I focus through the scope and set a target directly on the chest of the man closest to Kaleb. There are three men, and I know I could take them all within a few seconds. I just need the clear. We need to know what's inside that house and in the surrounding area. I get how Kase wants to make sure this all goes down like it's supposed to, but if one of these fuckers touches him, I'm shooting. I'll blow their fucking head right off their disgusting body and enjoy every minute of it.

They all seem to be talking and laughing like this is a joke. I watch them all walk up to Kaleb and keep watching as each one of them pull out their dicks like they're going to take a piss, all of them aiming at him. This is it. I'm fucking done, and I don't give two shits what anyone says. They are done torturing him. Their lives are over. I lower my scope and fire hitting him straight in the dick. Then I do it again. Before I can hit the third one, he turns away, so I hit him in his ass before he has the chance to take a step. They fall to the ground, and I hear pissed-off voices in my headphones as they scream for everyone to move now. *Fucking finally.*

I put the strap of my rifle over my shoulder and pull it tight against my body before I run straight for Kaleb. The others will have my back even though I hear them calling my name through my earpiece. I will not stand by and watch anyone piss on one of my guys, especially my guy.

As I get closer, I see our American flag spread across the ground below him, but my eyes are searching for movement from Kaleb. He's just hanging there, and my heart is screaming at his hopefully beating heart to show me he's alive. Give me a sign, Kaleb. Give me a fucking sign. Inhale, exhale. Scream in pain. Anything to let me know you're still here with me.

My footing is quick, and I jump over broken branches the entire way. I catch a glimpse of Harris to my right and speed up along with him. Two men exit the house, and I hear two shots echo through the air right after, so I'm only guessing there'll be more.

I don't stop to think. I'm aware I'm acting on impulse right now and a sniper shouldn't be running in like this. It's a good thing I'm good at many things. I draw my pistol to the front of my body and aim at the guy I shot in the ass trying to crawl away from Kaleb's feet. Sending a bullet straight through his head, I scan the other two for any movement, but they're not even trying to move. Good. Rot in hell, you sick fucks.

My focus is back on Kaleb as soon as my feet come to a stop. My eyes water at the sight of his wounds, and my heart hurts so fucking bad I can hardly move.

His head hangs low, and if I didn't recognize his tattoos, I'd never know this is him. He's been beaten beyond recognition, and an overwhelming rush of anger flows through my body.

Harris goes straight for Kaleb's restraints with his knife, working to free him, and I move in to hold his lifeless body. He's so cold. The night is hot, but he's cold. "Kaleb, baby. I'm here." My eyes race over him for any fucking sign he's still with me. "Please, god. Please, don't take him from me." Tears roll down my face, and I blink past them, trying to see him completely. Harris finally breaks the tension of the ropes, and his weight falls into my arms. It takes everything I have to hold him as I drag him a few feet from the bloody, piss-covered flag beneath him. Harris helps me with his heavy, lifeless body, and we both fall to the ground with him at the sound of gunshots at our backs. I check for his pulse on the side of his neck right away, and thank god, I find one.

"Fuck. Elliott. Tell me he's alive. I've got to kill these motherfuckers." Harris pulls out his gun and begins to fire toward the house.

"There's a heartbeat." My eyes land on his swollen lids, and I let my fingers brush his face. He's covered in mud, blood, blisters, and there are open wounds all over his body. I'm afraid to touch him, but I have to, so I keep my fingers near his neck. It seems to be the least injured, and through the sound of chaos I try to bring calm to him through my touch.

"Kaleb. Don't you dare leave me here. I need you. You promised me that fucking vacation." His eyelids flicker slightly, and I wish I could see his blue eyes. His lips move to say something, but nothing comes out.

The air is silent again, and Harris turns to look at Kaleb. He takes his shirt off and covers Kaleb's body in an attempt to spare him the embarrassment of this situation. Kaleb winces with every touch from us, and I start to worry how we'll ever get him out of here.

"Stay with me, brother." Harris runs his hand over Kaleb's forehead, and I hear the rustle of many boots approaching. The team is surrounding us now as they all watch the entire area, guns drawn and ready to fire at anything that moves.

"Fuck." The word comes out of his mouth as a near growl, but it comes out. Kaleb's swollen eyes pull together tighter, and I move closer to his ear.

"Please be strong. I promise to make it worth your while. We have so much left to do, Kaleb. Just stay with me." The guys start to talk behind me, and I catch the end of what they're saying.

"It's not a great plan, but it's a fucking plan. We need to get him the hell out of Mexico and to a hospital that can take care of him. He's going to need care here though. And probably a few days of recovery before we move him back to the States." Jackson and Kase crouch down behind me as I'm still lying beside Kaleb. Harris hasn't moved either, and we both work to cover him and protect him in case someone else is alive and tries to shoot him.

"The house is clear." Steele's voice rings through the night air, and I feel the guys relax just slightly. "I count twelve bodies. We're going to need to move now."

"The truck is five miles out. It'll be a few minutes," someone rumbles out.

"Stand watch so I can stabilize him." Bullet moves in and crouches as Harris stands to his feet. His determined eyes scan our surroundings, and I find comfort in knowing they're all on watch, while I focus on Kaleb.

I want to feel relieved I have Kaleb near me, but just looking at him, I can tell he's in so much pain.

"Alright, Ice. Move your ass. I need in here." I move to let Bullet inspect him. "Fuck." Bullet practically growls his frustration. The look on his face as he takes in all of Kaleb's injuries tells me what I already know. This is brutal.

CHAPTER SEVEN

KALEB

"Goddamn it, Kaleb, stay still." Fucking Bullet. "Where is she?" I cringe and damn near pass out from the pain shooting across my entire body.

"I'm right here." *Jade. Thank fuck.* I wish like hell I could see her clearly, but damn, I'm struggling to open my eyes. My lids are heavy and my vision is blurred. If I didn't hear my team rustling around, I would swear my head was half hanging off of my neck by the way it feels. I feel like shit. Like I'm halfway to hell and only the sound of her sweet voice is holding me back.

My mind drifts in and out. I'm conscious, then I'm not, but I know Jade is here.

"I'll carry his ass." I hear the deep rumbling of Jackson's voice.

I can't talk. My throat is raw and dry, and I'm fighting like I've never fought before to stay conscious, so I can be alert.

The last thing I remember before the beautiful sound of her voice and the sweet smell of gunpowder were my brother's threats.

Did they kill the piece of shit? Damn it, I need to know.

"He's stabilized, but hell, we have to get him to the hospital. Where the hell is Steele with that chopper?" Bullet is barking orders loudly, and I wish I had it in me to tell him to shut the fuck up, so I can hear her. He doesn't know how to tone down his voice when he's excited.

"Are you positive he's strong enough to make the trip? Or should we take him to a hospital here?" There she is. My brave girl. I need to see her to know if this is real, or if I'm hallucinating on my fucked-up trip to hell. I blink, trying to force my eyes open again. My eyes are drier than the damn desert we are in, but damn it, they open. Barely.

"Kaleb," she speaks softly. I continue to work my eyes up and down repeatedly until I'm staring into the eyes of the most stunning woman I will ever see in my life. She's a sight for these strained, sore eyes. A vision I've held on to since the last time I saw her up close.

"Fucking tell me this shit is real?" I bite out, only to go into a coughing fit that practically dislodges my windpipe from my lungs. "I'm right here. We all are. Don't try to talk." On a normal day, the warmth from her hand in mine would be enough to calm me down, but not tonight.

"I need water," I choke out. "There's some right here." I follow her movements with my eyes. I'll admit to anyone I'm scared to have her out of my sight. Knowing she's safe is all the medicine I need right now. Fuck going to the hospital.

Jade is calm and seems so delicate when she helps me lift my head, bringing a bottle of water to my lips. It's cold and feels good going down my throat, until I start coughing again. The small sips she's giving me keep dribbling down my chin.

"Baby, please. I can't imagine how you feel, but for me, close your eyes and rest. Steele should be here any minute. You're safe. I have you and we're going home." Call me a pussy, a dick, or a spineless bastard, I really couldn't give a fuck, but hearing her call me baby along with the love in her voice is enough for me not to argue with her.

Hell, one minute, my body feels the fire from every stinging strike from being whipped and punched, then the next, I feel like I'm lying naked in a tub of ice. I smile at the thought of the word ice. Her call name. I drift back to sleep, warm this time instead of freezing and shivering, because the next time I'm lying naked it sure as fuck isn't going to be hanging from a damn tree. It's going to be inside of her.

I wake from a nightmare, or is it reality? I'm not sure. Desperation sets in as I try to figure that out. I can't lift my arms or move my feet. "What the fuck?" I yell while I try to adjust my eyes to the blinding lights.

"Hey, calm down. You're going to be okay. We're back in the States in a hospital in San Antonio." Jade's once again at my side. Christ almighty. I've never wanted to see anyone like I do her now. She literally takes my breath away. Her hair is in a messy bun, and she has a little makeup on her face. Her low-cut tank top shows the cleavage to her perfect tits, and my fucking cock twitches in perfect timing to show me it still works after all the torture. Well, fuck, at least I know being hit and punched in my dick didn't break it. Now, I can say this is a dream come true, not a nightmare. I prayed for days to see her again, even if it was like this.

"I'm calm." I try to lift my hands up in surrender, but they won't budge.

"You have an IV in your arm. Stay still, damn it." She places my arm back straight and I wince slightly from the tightness of my skin. I'm all kinds of fucked up. Now that I'm awake, I have questions. A hell of a lot of them. Questions I'm not ready to ask yet because I'm afraid of the answers.

Plus, I don't want to interrupt her smell invading my nose. There were moments I thought I'd never see her again. Let alone have the chance to inhale her sensual smell. God, it sucks not to be able to move and touch her like I so badly want to. I'm desperate, half groggy, and one horny fucker with her this close to me.

"If you're my nurse, then I demand you take your clothes off." The look she gives me lets me know that isn't going to happen.

"I need to get the doctor in here." She stands, leaning over me, and those damn tits of hers are right in my face. I'm going to kill her for this. No, I take that back. I'm going to fuck those tits and tease her while I hold back a release from her on purpose, as a punishment for taunting me like this.

"What?" The innocent look on her face would make a normal man believe she has no idea what she's doing, but I'm not normal. Far from it.

"You put those tits in my face again, and I don't give a fuck if I'm in a hospital or not, nor do I care I have an IV in my arm. I'll rip the fucker out. Then I'll tear that barely-there shirt off of you and slide my cock between your tits. Then I'll glide it straight into your mouth, where you can say you're fucking sorry."

"I hate to break this to you, Sir. You won't be using that big dick of yours for a long time. Although," she leans in close, her shiny lips within a few inches of mine. "There's no need to try to get all alpha on me and punish me for anything. I'll glide you into my mouth without any encouragement from your pissed-off mouth." Before I can respond, a man in blue scrubs walks in.

"Glad to see you awake, Kaleb. I'm Doctor Weiss." He saunters in and sits in a chair on the opposite side of the bed from Jade with what I assume is my chart in his hand.

"Tell me when I can get the hell out of here." I'm assuming he's paying attention to Jade and not me by the way he's staring at her. If this little shit doesn't take his eyes off of my woman, wrapped up and bruised body or not, I'm going to beat his ass before I shove those nerdy glasses down his throat and stick my foot up his ass.

"Kaleb. You'll go home when you're healed and not a damn day before. Sorry about this grumpy ass here; he seems to have woken up without any manners. Please, carry on." She smiles at him, and I nearly growl. I'm lying here flat on my back, unable to move, and she's flirting with some jock of a doctor. Oh, hell no. I'll remember this, and when I do, I'll have her on her knees, begging for me to forget it.

At least I know I'm feeling better. I'm back to my barbaric ways when it comes to this woman. *Damn, Jade, you have no idea what you do to me.*

"It's fine, Mrs. Maverick. He's been through quite a bit." Mrs. Maverick? The doctor carries on, telling me all the bullshit I don't need to hear. I can feel where my injuries are. I felt every one of them as I endured that hell.

While I was out for almost a week, they have hydrated me and cleaned my wounds. I had to be stitched up in several places. They kept me knocked out just to help me tolerate the pain. Now that I'm coherent, they would like to test my pain tolerance to see if they need to increase my dosage or not. He continues on about every damn organ in my body, from my head to my toes. I'm trying to register what he's saying. However, the only thing I'm registering out of all of this is why the hell he addressed her as Mrs. Maverick.

"Where the hell are you going, Mrs. Maverick?" I ask Jade the second the doctor leaves the room. I love saying that. Although, Jade Maverick sounds better.

"You need to settle down. A lot of things have happened in the week you've been here." She smirks when she talks. Damn her, that jealousy I felt is gone. I need her lips on mine. She can fill me in later. Fuck everything else for a while. I've missed her.

"You need to kiss me," I demand and challenge her to come closer. I'm hurting all over, but something tells me Jade is all the medication I need. I push myself up, avoiding showing her how much anguish my body actually feels, while I grab her by the back of the neck and pull her in for a kiss I've been thinking about for far too long. The cord from my IV pulls my tight skin, but I don't give a shit. I need her oxygen to be able to breathe.

Her lips are soft and she smells delicious. I could kiss her entire body right now. She slowly moves her tongue over my lips, and I still to a completely frozen state just to let her slowly kiss me. We remain face-to-face, and both of us open our eyes to look deep into each other's. I know I look like shit to her, but I can feel her looking into me. She feels what I feel inside, and this is the first time in my life I've felt this kind of connection with someone. I let my eyes move over her and internally thank god for letting me touch her once more.

Civilian casual looks so good on her. I know she's lost sleep and has been worried about me, but honestly, after everything I've been through, she couldn't look bad to me. But shit, if she's not so far from that side of the scale and causing all sorts of craziness in my heart. It's amazing to want something so bad that it's the very thing that keeps you alive. I've got my chance with her, and as I close my eyes and softly kiss her again, I know I'll do anything for her. Anything. I had no idea how hard I had fallen for her until I was held hostage. I knew she had gotten to me, but the shit I was thinking about while hanging from that tree was far from the realm of possibilities in my mind before Mexico.

"I love you, Jade." She sits back and looks at me, not saying a word as I continue. I run my hand down her arm and try to say the right words to let her know just how much I need her. "You saved me out there."

"I tried."

"No, you did. It was you I talked to every time I spoke, even if it was all just in my own head. I felt you there with me. I knew you were hurting, and I kept fighting because I knew you wanted me to. You gave me a reason to stay, Jade." A small tear slides down her cheek, and I move to stop it. This is supposed to be a great fucking day, and I'm in here, making her cry.

"Kaleb. You scared me. I thought I had lost you, and my heart hurt so damn bad. I can't deal with losing you like that." She's whimpering now, and I can tell she's on the verge of breaking down. It kills me seeing her like this.

"You won't have to. I'm not going anywhere for a very long time. I'm going on a very long fucking vacation and plan to take you with me as soon as I can break out of here." That draws a smile from her gorgeous face.

"You know I'll have to go back soon. I've talked to my superior several times. I'm good with more R&R, considering everything that's happened, but I do have to report in when we get back. I guess there's a shit ton of paperwork before I can do anything. I'll have to do that, and then we can go from there. They know it's been a rough several weeks, so I'm good for a few more if we stay local in the States for sure. I'm not being called to duty for at least a month." I can't comprehend that right now. I don't want to talk about what we'll do when that happens. It doesn't matter when it is, I won't be ready to let her go.

"I know you do, but I promised you a trip and we are taking one." Maybe if I sound demanding enough, it'll work.

"How about Bali?" Holy shit, that sounds perfect. Of course, I'd say anything is perfect compared to this hospital in southern Texas.

"Tell Kase, and he'll get us out of here. That fucker can plan anything."

"That is very romantic. Have your friend plan our trip, while you just lie around here and bark orders." There's my sarcastic girl. She smiles and leans in for another kiss, and I watch her soften again before my eyes. She runs her fingers through my hair and pulls her mouth from mine, allowing only about an inch of space between us.

"Kaleb Maverick. Fire. Commander. Sir. Whatever it is you want me to call you. I love you too." There's a knock at the door, interrupting her, but she kisses me once more before she stands. "And if you ever fuck around on me, I'm going to shoot you in the dick just like I did those other guys. So think about that as you move forward from here." I watch her ass through my swollen eyes and smile. That's my ass. That's my woman. Even with that feisty fucking mouth, I wouldn't change one single thing about her.

CHAPTER EIGHT

JADE

Whoever is behind that knock on the door has the worst timing. There's more to be said between the two of us. Kaleb needs to talk. He needs to tell me what he remembers. The mere idea of him having to relive the savage things done to him sends another sharp spear of anxiety that lies dormant in the center of my chest. I've worked out the details with my superior. Thank god, they don't have me training or scheduling me for a mission as of yet. Our time off could be days or weeks at a time. I do have to check in daily or report to work in other areas when I'm not deployed, but I was granted personal time off because of what I've been through in the past few weeks.

I've been sitting by his side for almost a week, talking and pleading with him to come back to me. Crying. Me, Jade Elliott, whose heart used to be hard as a block of ice until he brought his fire into my life and melted it. I've cried more times in the past week than I can remember throughout my entire life. All over this man I'm in love with.

Even though anxiety is consuming my body, I can honestly say I don't feel the need to take a pill to calm me. Knowing Kaleb is safe is all I need. Love is the bond and the strength to get a person through anything, especially when it's this obvious it's mutual.

Love, a word never on my radar, has now taken over my existence. My world revolves around this man.

I'm in love with him because of the deep connection I've felt with him from the second I laid eyes on him. Dealing with the torture of this week has only intensified my feelings towards him. My mind went crazy, thinking of everything he went through, as I examined all of the marks on his body. I can tell he was whipped many times. The wounds are starting to heal, but I'm afraid the surface scars will always be there. And I don't even want to think about the internal scars something like this would bring.

I don't care what he looks like or how much this will torment him. He takes me and I take him just the way he is. He's been point blank about wanting me from the first day we met, and now it's time I match his determination. His blastoff introduction to have me on my knees that first day could've so easily gone a different way. I'm just glad I felt the connection the second I laid eyes on him.

I shove these feelings aside as I make my way to the door. I swing it open, only to be swept off of my feet by Jackson.

"We heard the princess is awake." He comes barreling in, followed by everyone else. I could laugh right now at the term Jackson used to address Kaleb, but I won't. That's Jackson's story to tell.

"This princess is going to turn into an evil queen if you don't get your filthy hands off of my woman. Now, motherfucker."

I laugh. Right along with everyone else when they all stroll in with their big bodies, filling this small room to the brink where I actually smell testosterone over the bitter odor of the disinfectant I've been smelling for days.

"She's a hell of a lot lighter than you are." Placing me back down on the floor, Jackson winks then goes to Kaleb, who raises his brows in uncertainty.

"Man. You look a hell of a lot better than the last time we saw you. You holding up okay?" Harris, my rock for the past few days, stretches out his arm to shake Kaleb's hand. He takes it, and their eyes meet. Kaleb says thank you, while Harris replies with his welcome.

"I'm good. Ready to get the hell out of here."

"We'll make it happen. Before we go, brother, you need to fill us in. We need to know what the hell happened to you. I'm not asking you to relive the hell they put you through. I'm asking if you know any of those motherfuckers. You kept talking in your sleep, and we're all trying to figure out what's going on here. Did they manage to break you and get any information?" It's Kase who's blunt and straight to the point.

"Do I look like they broke me? I'm still alive, fuckers. Of course, they didn't break me. I would've died first, and all of you know that."

"We've got the President up our asses. These two have the Army up theirs. This is all kinds of fucked up." He points to both Harris and I. I'm about ready to tell him to calm down. That Harris and I are fine with our commanding officers. Yes, they want us back, but they know we need to be ready before we go back in.

This isn't common behavior. We aren't civilians like the rest of these guys. Our call of duty hasn't been completed, but we're a team, and one of our men has been injured. Not to mention, he happens to be the man I love. The Army gets this, whether it's right or wrong or even the proper way things are done. None of that matters. We've been briefed and our statements have been documented. This is our time. Our leave. We earned it.

What none of them know, though, not even Harris, is the minute I return, I'm going to do everything in my power to be put on this team for every mission from here on out. I've had too many days to dwell on this decision while staring into the blank, beaten face of the man I love. The only time I left here was to be briefed by a Sergeant Major from Lackland Air Force Base and shop for some damn clothes and necessities I needed until we get out of here.

My heart wants a life with Kaleb. After this and the killing of the boy in Afghanistan, I can't worry about either one of us being away without the other. He'll be thrilled about this; I know he will. Danger is part of this job. Worry will claw away at him, like it did me, if we're apart. He may be a hardass, but the man knows how hard I've worked for this. I deserve to be with Kaleb and he deserves to be with me. Everyone knows we work well together. The opposite is not in the cards for me. To have either one of us out in this world not knowing where the other one is will only tear us up every damn second. I'm not going through this again. I can't.

I've proven my loyalty and dedication to my country. I'd lay my life down to protect it. I've earned the right to be heard and to make what I feel is one simple request. Just put me alongside Kaleb on special missions, where I can shine like the true sniper I've worked so hard to be.

I know we'll have to work hard at our relationship too. I'm not an idiot. Maverick is one difficult man, but I can be just as difficult. Not to mention the kind of missions his team will go on, but it will keep me in the mix of doing what I love. It's actually a better fit for me. Get in, fuck shit up, and then get out. Short missions that need my expertise. At least with this team, I'm not fighting against the Army's rules about a female Ranger going out on an active mission.

Kaleb and I will fight, there's no doubt about that, especially for control. We will struggle, but the one thing we've never had an issue with is communicating with each other. Both of us are outspoken, and we have no problem saying what's on our mind. We tell each other the way it is, and there is no one I'd rather climb into a doghouse with after fighting. I've always thought the Army was my dream. The day I met Kaleb Maverick was the day I realized I want more out of my life. I want him in it every single day.

I snap out of my thoughts when Kaleb tries to adjust the bed himself. Frustration blows from his lips, only filling the room with more testosterone.

"Let me help." I go to him and place my hand under his head while I push the button to slowly lift him into a higher sitting position. He hisses and swears like crazy, causing my heart to shatter. I know he's fighting the pain and is desperately trying to stay alert. He has another thing coming if he thinks I'm going to stand here and watch him suffer. As soon as we're done here, he's receiving more meds, even if it knocks him out for a few hours. After all, they think I'm his wife. Which we haven't discussed either.

"Son of a bitch." He catches his breath. Short gasps escape his mouth.

"Brother. We can do this later," Steele says sympathetically.

"Fuck that. I'm good. I want this done. You may all want to park your asses on the floor before you fall." He grabs my hand, tugging me down to sit on the side of the bed. Something is off with him. In a way I've never seen before. A mixture of hurt, pain, and disgust breaks across his handsome face.

With another tug, he draws me next to him on the bed. My fingers slip delicately around his. He's scaring me. His hold on my fingers increases to the point of pain as he prepares himself to speak. It's as if he needs me to be his anchor right now. I have no clue what's rattling around in his head, but wonder if it's memories or visions of his brutal attack.

Not even his strong fingers around mine prepare me for what he tells us.

"It was my brother Ty who did this to me." His muscled stomach rises and falls through the thin cotton of the hospital gown after he speaks. He refuses to let me go. The need for me to look into his eyes weighs heavy on my heart. I do everything I can to hide my negative reaction to this news. This is killing him. With every breath he takes, I feel his heart thump harder and faster. I can't imagine how he feels, what he's thinking, or god, the heartache he must've felt to be abused, taunted, and have his heart tossed into a damn blender by someone who should love him. This makes me sick.

And no wonder he hasn't said a damn thing about this having to do with his brother. From what little he told me, he's a drug user, who has never gotten his life together. A sick excuse of a man, who has done nothing but bring heartache to his own mother and family.

"Jesus Christ. You have to be shitting me, man. That's where he ran off to? It wasn't enough he pumped every goddamn poison out there into his veins? Is he selling the shit now too? And to top it off, he took this shit out on you? Is that what the hell is happening here? Fucking hell. I'm going to murder that lowlife motherfucker." I jump as Pierce's hatred escapes him, his jaw clenching tight as he paces the floor, wearing his anger on his face.

I've never seen him react to anything like this before. Not when Kaleb was taken from us. Not when we all saw him hanging from that tree. I don't know the man well, but he does not strike me as the kind of guy to lose control. I can't speak for fear I'm going to mesh my words with tears. Kaleb squeezes me harder.

How ironic the phrase 'Life can change in a blink of an eye' is. Life will gut you, spit you out, and leave you hanging on the edge of a cliff. Kaleb is dangling there right now. A moment ago, this room was filled with our outpouring of love for another. And now, it is filled with hatred for a man so evil that blood or not, he is not Kaleb's brother. His true brothers are all in this room.

"Kaleb." I push off the bed, using the strength in my feet, unable to look at him right now. Instead, I look to Harris, who looks almost defeated. All of them do as I scan their faces one by one. Someone needs to say something other than spitting angry words out. How the hell I've all of a sudden become the sensible one here beats me. I'm usually the hardass, the bitter bitch, but shit, we need to find out if we killed that asshole. If Kaleb's brother is dead. I have to ask, whether it hurts him more or not.

"Does anyone know if he was one of the men we took out the other night?" I hate to be blunt, especially when I know that no matter what has happened in the past between Kaleb and his brother, he has to still love him. To have your own family try to kill you has to be one of the most devastating, emotional turmoils to have to deal with.

"I got the footage from when I scanned the area. All of our recordings can be watched to see if we can locate him as one of the fuckers we killed." Pierce stands wider as I can see his thoughts running through his head. He's hungry for this to be the case. I don't know if I hope I shot him in his dick, or if he was the one who got the ass shot and then a bullet to his head. Either way, I hope he's gone. I hope he took a bullet through his black-as-coal heart. Anyone who can do something like this to Kaleb should be dead and rotting in the farthest recess of hell, as far as I'm concerned.

"Great. I was hoping to relive that moment over and fucking over. Don't get any bright ideas about teasing me about that shit. I'll repay your asses in a way that'll make your dicks draw up and hide." Kaleb looks at all the guys before he begins to tell us everything he remembers. While I remain still, while anger and sadness pound away at my bleeding heart.

CHAPTER NINE
KALEB

I can't share every fucking detail that happened. There's no way I'm telling these guys, or hell, Jade for that matter, about the depth of the shit my brother put me through. I pissed him off when I fought back and head butted him. He was out for a few minutes. Then my life became hell. I decided in that moment I wasn't going to try that again unless I knew I could kill him. He beat me so bad I passed the hell out, never once waking up until I realized I was being saved.

I hold on tight to Jade's hand. She's tense and I hate this. This room is claustrophobic as fuck too. I'm in so much pain, it's hard to breathe, but I'm working through the words that seem to be practically choking me, lodging themselves there, because, Christ, even though this shit happened to me, every damn thing I say will make each one of these men and the woman I love feel like it happened to them. I care too much to put them through a nightmare that will repeat itself in their heads. There's no end. I'll remember this shit for all eternity. It will be bad enough to witness seeing myself hanging lifeless. My nudity and busted-up body for everyone in this room to see will embed itself into the memories for the rest of their lives.

"I'm not sure where to start. I mean, the fucker tortured me in ways I'll never talk about. Then my piece of shit brother rolled in and made it personal. He threatened my mom, my sister, and tried to get me to react about Jade." *Fuck.*

The way Harris instantly stares me down in his big brother protective way makes me want to shove those last words back in my mouth. I should've known he'd be on high alert when it comes to her. I won't let that bother me anymore, because honestly, knowing he was with her in Mexico calmed me. I knew she was safe with him.

"What the fuck? How does he know about her?" Harris is tense and in a fight stance as he responds to only the beginning of my story. If we hadn't had our talk about my feelings for Jade and for the fact I know damn well something happened between him and Mallory by the way she fucked him with her eyes the night before I left his ranch, I would say he still wants her. Harris cares about her. They've been through a lot together, but she's like family to him. Like my brothers here are to me. So I get why he's protective of her.

"He was guessing. I didn't show any proof she's fucked up my heart." She looks surprised that I'm sharing this with the guys, and I smile with as much enthusiasm as I can handle. She needs to loosen up. Besides, I'd love nothing more than to tease her and play all fucking night, but the truth of it is, I'm still fucking hurting.

"Watch out there, big guy, with talk like that, you'll be married before you know it." Jackson steps in with his smartass Southern drawl.

"Who knows? I could think of worse things, that's for sure." They all just stare at me like I've lost my mind. That's okay, because I did out there. Jade hasn't told me why the doctor called her Mrs. Maverick yet. My guess is, she had to with all the red tape that goes along with the privacy acts our country has. But I'm not concerned about that shit. They can call her any damn thing they want as long as it implies she's mine.

"I listened to them talk and tried to make out as many words as I could. They run guns and drugs. My brother was the lead out there, but he answered to someone. He made phone calls within hearing distance of me, I'm sure thinking I would never make it out of there alive." Her grip on my fingers tightens as I watch their reactions. *Fuck, I don't want to talk about this shit.*

"Somehow, he got in with the Mexican Cartel and worked his way up the ranks. I'm thinking they must be trading guns for the transport and protection of Al-Quaren, and when we fucked that up, it fucked up their next row of shipments."

I begin to recall a specific conversation from one of the lost days out there. "He was getting his ass chewed about it and tried to talk himself out of some deep shit with whomever he works under."

Shit, that feels like an hour ago, but it's nearly been a week. I move my arm to adjust my body and am reminded of the soreness. I'm very aware the pain meds are wearing off. Thank fuck they knocked me out when they moved me, because I don't know how I could've coped with it coherent.

"So, we fucked up his little life by kidnapping the piece of shit we captured. I see how this pissed him off. Why does that make me want to fucking smile?" Bullet knows the shit my brother has done in the past. Hell, he was around when it went from bad to worse with Ty and my mom. He was the one who helped protect my sister when I knew that fucking brother of mine would hurt her just to get to me.

"That we did. He told me that himself. He was pushing for the location of Al-Quaren. That's all he cared about." The tap on the door stops me mid-thought. A hot little nurse walks in, and I feel the tension in the room grow. Shit, these assholes are going to make her life hell for the three minutes she'll be in here.

"I need to get your vitals and check your chart. It's time for your meds again." She walks in innocently, and they all part to clear a path for her to reach me before they circle her back in. With the way their eyes are bulging out of their heads, you'd think they've gone a year without pussy.

Jackson will be the first to flirt. That's how he works. Shit, I have never been happier in my life, anticipating what these guys are going to do. I could use a good laugh.

"You going to need him to turn his head and cough? I think you should check everywhere. Make him bend over." She smiles like she's never been harassed before as Jackson's deep voice fills the room.

"Not today. I think we're going to let him rest." Thank fuck for that. I'm sure my cock has been handled by several women while I was out. Not the one I desperately want to be handling it though. The fucker twitches at the mere thought of Jade's mouth wrapped around him. *This is not the damn time to decide you're in functioning order,* DICK. I have Jackson's next words spilling out of his arrogant, mouthy ass to thank for pulling my mind away from my own dick.

"Great. You know, I think I need someone to examine me. Maybe play a little nurse and check my heart rate under stress." He crosses his arms and stands proud. She watches me as she gets near and glances at Jade with a slight grin on her face before she listens to my chest through her stethoscope.

"I can arrange that. Nurse Rocko will be in shortly and has some free space in his wing." Her brows rise when she speaks, and I can see on her face that she likes him. Well, shit hasn't changed around here. He's not called 'Action Jackson' for nothing. Even though I know the real reason why he's called that, I'll keep it to the down low, for now. Talk like that would never work for me. Hell, Jade would truly have my ass examined by the guy with the biggest fucking hands in the hospital just to prove a point. The nurse hands me my pills and a cup of water. Against what my mind is telling me, I swallow them down, knowing my body has been through enough. I need to rest and let my body heal.

"Fuck that Rocko nurse. I'll wait until you're off shift. I'd feel better keeping this private and use Maverick's nursing staff, since this was such a dangerous mission and all." She smiles at him as she passes and hands him the piece of paper she scribbled on. Her number, no doubt. I'm sure he just got the time and place too. She leaves the room and we all bust out laughing at him. That asshole is smooth. How women fall for that shit is beyond me.

"Jackson, seriously. Is that your pickup style? Because if so, I'd kick your ass." Jade stands beside me and stretches her arms over her head. I watch her tits as she does and wish like hell I could actually appreciate them properly.

"It fucking worked." He holds up the paper. "Darlin', it's my voice. I could say any fucking thing I want and panties just drop. They love how deep it is." Then he gyrates his hips forward, thrusting the air a few times.

"I think I'm going to be sick." Steele grabs his stomach playfully.

"I am sick," Harris digs in. The room fills with laughter and I can't help but join in. That is, until a sharp pain has me wanting to roll over in a fetal position. Fuck. As much as I want to be better, I'm still fucked up.

"Kaleb." Jade's worried expression calms me, knowing how much she cares. I hate the fact I'm lying here, helpless, unable to do a damn thing. I'd love nothing more than to run my fingers across her furrowed forehead and ease the ache I know she's feeling inside. God. I love her. After my first taste of her, I told myself she would be the one to break me. She has.

CHAPTER TEN

KALEB

"Hey, handsome." My sexy, blond beauty walks in with some real food. I've been drugged up and recuperating for a little over two weeks now in this hospital. The food sucks, and my ass is killing me from lying in this stiff bed. My muscles ache from not working out, and my cock aches even more from not getting its own workout. Especially now, when I take a good look at her gorgeous smile.

"Jesus, Jade." I snatch the bag out of her hand. The whiff of cheeseburger assaults my nose, making my stomach cry out.

"I'm sorry I'm late. I told you I had to stop at the hotel the guys are staying at to shower and change." Her hands go to her hips. My hands should be on those hips while I'm slamming into her sweet pussy from behind.

"I'm talking about the way you look." Taking a big bite of my juicy burger, I look down her body before allowing my eyes to move back up. This damn burger has to be the second best thing I've tasted in my life. She looks down at her jean shorts, and I see why they call them shorts. They leave nothing to the imagination at all.

"You're sexually frustrated and an asshole. Eat that damn thing before the doctor and the guys get here so we can go home." Her fine ass walks to the other side of the room. She picks up my clothes along with an American flag before she starts packing them all into a bag. I found out a few days after arriving here that my brother and his fuckhead followers laid our country's flag down at my feet and pissed on it.

Ty has not only become a traitor to our country, but he placed the flag, the one item we pledge our American freedom to, in the dirt and defiled it. He should die for that alone.

I finish my burger, crumpling up the paper loudly to drag her attention back to me.

Her head snaps around. *She's so fucking beautiful.*

"I know you, baby. You going to stand over there and tell me you don't want my cock?" I lift my brows, knowing damn well she's as frustrated as I am. We've both discussed this over the course of the last week, while I faded in and out from the pain medicine I finally caved into letting the doctors give me that first day I woke up. My skin burned so damn bad, I felt like they were beating me all over again. Yet I still pissed and moaned about fucking her mouth, her pussy, her ass. I may have been drugged up, but I'm not blind. I saw the way she squirmed in the chair and crossed her legs over one another. She wants it.

"I've been taking care of myself," she taunts.

Before I can tell her that no one, not even she, should be touching her body in any goddamn way unless I'm watching her, the doctor walks in. Followed by Kase, Pierce, and Jackson. The others went home. Not everyone needs to sit here all day, watching me sleep, doing absolutely nothing. We still haven't watched the footage. I asked them to wait until I could get the hell out of here.

I have no idea if Ty is alive or not. Which is partially why the others went home. I wanted extra security for my mom and sister. I'm not taking his threats lightly, not when it comes to two of the three women who mean more to me than my own damn life. They've both had security on them for years. It goes with my job, but now it's tripled.

One of the guys I served two tours with owns a security firm in Atlanta. I need to call him to thank him for helping me out. He sent a crew to watch my mom's house and another one to watch my sister during the day while she works. Hell, I was too weak to even hold a phone when that call needed to be made a few weeks ago. I owe Kase for taking care of that for me without me even needing to ask. Hell, he's stepped up to the plate big time. He even took it upon himself to stock my fridge at the compound with food for when we get home today. Fucking perfect because I plan to eat like a beast until I'm back to normal. My body is withering away with this bullshit food in here.

I haven't talked to my mom or sister yet. As far as they know, I'm off doing my job. The first thing I'm gonna do when I get home is talk to them. I may be a grown man, but we all need to hear the sound of our mom's voice every now and then.

"You ready to get your ass out of here, brother?" Kase asks when he steps to the side of the bed, bringing me out of my mind.

"He can leave whenever he wants." My doctor, who I still want to punch, speaks with authority. His eyes are trained on Jade's ass. Hello, fucker. Your patient is over here. I'll make sure she gets what she needs.

"Great, then. Take care of yourself. Make sure you set that appointment up with your doctor back home, Mr. Maverick."

"Will do." I swing my legs around before he finishes speaking. I've been dressed and ready to go since they told me this morning I'd be able to get the hell out of here.

I grab Jade's hand, while Jackson tugs my bag from around her shoulder. I'd sure as fuck like to say I walked out of this place, but hell, no. In strides Jackson's sexy little nurse walks in. He's spent a shit ton of time with her the past few days and now she's pushing a goddamn wheelchair to haul my ass out of here.

"I'll call you when we land." Jackson places a kiss on the top of his latest victim to the 'action team.' I mock him in my head. He's so full of shit. He won't call her. She was his distraction for the week he stayed down here. He knew he'd never see her again after we left. I know him. It's what he does. That's the only reason why he spent so much time with her. He says it just isn't the same after you've hit it a few times. Claims he likes variety.

"Sure," she tells him as she steps back so both Jackson and Pierce can help me slide my slow-moving body into the back of a van.

"A fucking minivan." I about die laughing. It's one hell of a sight to the people we pass on the way to the airport as they look once, then do a double take, their heads turning when they see three big-ass men and one badass woman in a green, ugly as fuck minivan.

Thank fuck the flight to the compound is a short one. Sitting next to Jade in this private plane Pierce arranged is killing me. I've adjusted my cock more times than I can count. It's been hard since I trailed behind her climbing the set of stairs to get inside the cabin.

My body is still mangled and bruised, but I'll be damned if that's going to stop me from sliding inside the tightest, sweetest pussy I've had.

The minute I hang up with my mom and sister, I'm all over her ass. Goddamn, I may have to take her ass again. Not tonight. Soon though. My legs are still fucked all to hell. *Shit.* I tilt my head back in my seat and train my hard glare out the window while I dread that fucking phone call.

What the hell am I going to say to my mom? I can't tell her the truth, legally anyway. Besides, the truth would kill her. She hides her pain well, or at least she has over the years. I know it's to protect Amelie and I. All these years, she's lived with losing her son. A man who has now threatened to physically hurt her.

How in the fuck can he think the way he does? Maybe he isn't thinking at all. Maybe the fucker is dead. I hope like hell I see his lifeless body on that tape. Seeing his eyes wide open in shock right before he took his last breath would actually bring me relief.

"You okay over there?" Jade nestles into me, carefully. She needs to knock that shit off. I don't need her taking it easy on me anymore. I need her tough interior back. The smart-mouthed woman who has brought me to my damn knees over and over needs to make an appearance.

"I'm good. Just thinking about what I'm going to tell my mom. I thought I knew what I was going to say to her about the extra security I've put on her, but right now, it's bothering me. I know I can't tell her the truth. I just pray like hell she can't hear the lies in my voice. She's good at picking up on shit." It takes strength to not turn and look at her when I speak. I'm sick and damn tired of seeing pain mixed with anger, fear, and all kinds of bullshit when I look at Jade.

This is all too much. *Fuck.* I want that son of a bitch to be dead so damn bad and to get my life back on track. It's time I finally fucking get to live. I don't want to be scared I'm going to be sent off somewhere and get a call or return home to find out that monster has done something to my family. Fuck him for making me feel like a pussy out there. There's a part of me that hopes he isn't dead so I can kill him myself.

"Hey. Look at me, Kaleb." Jade laces her fingers through mine and whispers softly into my ear. I look at her, like she requests. This time, there is no fear. It's unconditional love staring back at me.

"If he's not on that tape, you know we'll get him. As far as your mother, I'll go and stay with her if that will make you feel better. It's time I meet her anyway. This woman who has made you into the man you are. The man I love." She's right about one thing. We will get him. However, she is wrong if she thinks I'm letting her out of my sight. I'm a selfish man when it comes to her. I've found happiness with this spitfire of a woman. She's the one who gave me strength to hang on to in the darkness. She gave me a reason to live. I would have given up so hell no, she isn't going anywhere, except tied to my bed, and I mean that literally.

"I appreciate that. But fuck, no." Her eyes soften even more from my hard stare. She gets me. She knows why I need her by my side. I have to have her near me for many reasons, but right now, I want to fuck her. Plain and simple. I want to bury my face between her legs and scrape my beard across her muscled thighs, and have her ride my cock until we both get that release we're craving.

"It was worth a shot." She shrugs and I slide my hand slowly up her stomach and over her chest. I pinch her nipple as

I brush over it, and she gasps. Her inhale literally lights my insides, and we both know I'm far from done. This is the beginning of what I have planned for her. I continue until I have a firm hold of the back of her neck, tugging her into my hard body. Thank god the guys aren't looking or paying any attention to what I'm about to tell her.

"I'm going to fuck you hard. It's going to hurt. We've both been through hell these past few weeks. I'm on edge and you've been scared. The way I see it, it's the only way to work that out of our systems. I need to pull your hair and take that sweet ass. I want to fuck your mouth, and god knows I'm burning to get deep inside that sweet pussy. I want it furiously. I want it hard. So hell no, you are not going anywhere except to my bed." My grip loosens on her neck. I look down at her and there she is. Her glare is tempting as she matches my fierce desire. If I didn't know her like I do, I'd be frightened I'd scare her away talking to her like this. I wait while she gets her labored breathing under control. I know it's coming. I welcome it.

"Sir, yes sir. But Kaleb, don't make me wait for days before I feel you again." Good god almighty. I fucking love this woman. That's it. I can't take another fucking second of this torture. I'm a needy man when it comes to sex, and I've been restricted. I don't do well with limits and boundaries.

"Get that sexy ass to the very back of the plane. I don't give a fuck if we have to do it on a seat, but I can't wait another fucking second." She looks at me with a smile on her face and worry in her eyes.

"Are you sure you're ready?"

"Fuck, yes, I'm ready. Go." Just like all the other times we were together, she causes this urgency inside me that just makes me want to fuck her for days. It's ridiculous how consumed I get, just like I am right now. We're going to fuck on an airplane with part of the team possibly watching, and I don't give two fucks. I just want her in my lap with my cock buried deep inside her.

I watch her sexy ass walk down the small aisle and actually thank god out loud when she opens a door to a small room with a full-sized bed. With one hand, I rip the fucking black comforter off and toss it to the floor.

"Kaleb. I don't want to hurt you." She's worried about hurting me? Fuck. I'm about ready to show her exactly what the word hurt means, in the most pleasurable way.

"Stop. I fucking need you to remember I'm a damn man. I'm not a goddamn pussy. You ride me. I'm dying to see those tits bounce in my face."

"Kaleb. Fucking stop." She has a pissed-off look on her face, and my cock is already rock hard waiting for this, so I hope like hell she's not about to tell me no. My eyes soften with hers, and I lower my head until we're eye to eye. My voice is deep and my words come out soft even though I feel like I'm being choked.

"Jade. I need this. I need to feel you again. You've been driving me crazy. You're the only thing I could think of out there. I told myself that if I ever had the chance to hold you again, I'd never let you go." She slides her arms around my waist and tucks her head against my chest. There's no doubt she can feel my heart racing as I try to calm it down on an exhale. I place my lips on her head and kiss her hair. I have to inhale her scent. She's so fucking intoxicating.

"I love you, Jade. I don't mean to seem insensitive, but right now, I just want to feel you. Show me how much you missed me." And with that, she takes a step back and raises her shirt over her head. With a quick reach behind her back, she's dropped her black lace bra to the floor and begins working her shorts and her little black panties down her long legs until she's tormenting me even more. They hit the floor at her feet and she steps out of them leaving them with her shoes. She's completely naked, waiting for me to make a move. She's all mine and knowing that makes me the happiest man alive.

"Kaleb Maverick. Please let me show you how much I've missed you." She slowly opens the buttons on my shirt then slides it over my shoulders with care. She places soft kisses over my shoulders and is extremely cautious with the bandage across my lower back. "You see. I go crazy if I see you're being hurt. I won't be the one to hurt you by not taking care of these wounds. If we do this... We have to be careful."

"Jade Elliott. I'll give you your calm sex now, but one day soon... I'm going to fuck you until you're damn sore. Hell, we'll both be sore, and I won't give a shit if it hurts us both to walk for days." Or crawl. Or never climb out of bed again. I'm ok with that fate.

"I look forward to that." She moves to face me, and I trace my fingers along her neck, down to her nipples. I brush over the peaks and watch them perk up to the hardness I missed feeling.

She unbuttons my pants and slowly works them down until I can step out of them with ease. "Now, lie down, so I can take care of you." I obey, but fight myself to let her have this control. I'll do it just this one time.

I watch her as she moves over me, continuing to kiss across my skin while she positions herself on my hips. My cock is standing hard, but she sits just in front of it, allowing it to bump up against her ass.

"I missed you. When they pulled the chopper up, my heart sank because I thought I'd never see you again." I see a tiny tear begin to fall down her right cheek, and it takes everything in me to not take over and show her just how fine I am.

"I'm here now, Jade. I heard you, and that's the reason I had hope out there. I wanted to feel this with you again." I pull her hand over my heart, and we look into each other's eyes while it beats into her palm. She literally holds my heart now, so I can't think of a more perfect way to start this.

I reach up, slide my hand through her hair, and guide her lips down to mine. Her kiss is soft and gentle, and it's almost like we're kissing each other for the first time. She places her hands beside my head and manages to continue kissing me without touching a single one of my bandages. Perfect. This, I can live with.

She rolls her hips up then slides gently onto my cock, and I exhale loudly the entire time I can feel her around me. "Am I hurting you?"

"Fuck, no. Keep going. You feel so good on my dick." She moves slowly up and down, raising her body into a sitting position. Her tits move as she does and I don't know where I want to put my hands the most, so I spread them over her chest and then move them over her body from there.

She's so fucking gorgeous. Her teeth nip on her bottom lip when I rotate my hips into her. The restraint I have that's keeping me from grabbing her hips and pounding into her over and over is insane. I've lost my goddamn mind over her.

She moves up and down on me until I can see her concentration shift. She's close. It's time I handle this shit for her.

I slide my thumb between us and splay my hand over her pelvis. With her clit under the pressure of my thumb, I roll that tender ball of nerves until she loudly takes her release from me and grinds herself harder as she goes.

I watch her eyes. She's trying to watch me, but loses the battle when her release rushes over her. Her moans are loud enough to be heard out in the cabin, and I love that she didn't even try to hold back. I want her to always give me her all.

She starts to move over me again. We both feel the plane descending and look at each other, knowing our time is limited. She lifts herself off of me, sliding down my body until she covers my cock with her mouth. I growl when her warmth covers me. Christ, look at her. She's making sure she pleases me and has no idea she already does in a way no one else can.

She takes me as deep as she can, trying to keep from gagging. Then she swallows, and I feel it at the tip of my cock. I swear that was a direct switch for me to come inside of her.

"Jade. I have to do this right. I want to be inside you the first time I come again. Come here, baby." I grab her shoulders to get her back on my dick. Her eyes grow wide with mischief, and she lets out a little groan when I slam her back down onto my cock. It only takes a few more thrusts into her hot center and I'm coming deep inside her just as the plane lands on the ground.

It was rough, but I wouldn't have wanted to land any other way.

"I love you. Remember, whatever you see on those tapes…. That I love you and I'm here for you." She kisses me on my cheek, and I grab the back of her head to guide her lips even closer to mine. We kiss for what seems like ten minutes without a care in the world. I know he others are all already off the plane. In fact, if I weren't so eager to see those tapes, I'd start on her again.

It's different now that I know I have a long time with her. Before, I had to push for more every time we were together. Now, I can relax, knowing she'll be by my side when shit gets handled.

"I love you too, Jade. I'm not sure what I hope to see on those tapes." She climbs off me and starts to get dressed.

"We'll deal with whatever it is." I watch her every move until she's covered, then bend to get my own clothes. I work my pants over the one bandage on my right thigh. I'm thankful I survived that hell, let alone being able to live a normal life. I know my brother didn't take it easy on me. I'm guessing he knew inflicting pain on my body wouldn't be true torture for me. My women would be the best way to get to me, and he fucking knew that.

I smooth my hair and beard just before I open the door, expecting an empty bird. Instead, I open it to Pierce and Jackson finalizing the information with the pilots in the main cabin. *Fuck.*

"Nice of you two to provide the music for our flight. I rather enjoyed that." Jackson's ass would be the one to listen in.

"Did you learn something, asshole?" This is the first time he's had a chance to listen in on me fucking someone. I've never been one to be so needy I couldn't wait until I was in the privacy of my own house, but Jade has changed that. She's changed me. I'm not sure I'll ever get enough of her.

"Ice sounds like she can handle the big, bad Fire all by herself." He smiles and fake punches her in the shoulder. She instantly punches him in the side to retaliate and gives him her own hell.

"Jackson. That's what it sounds like when a girl is satisfied. I can talk you through a woman's main pleasure points if you need me to." He laughs at her comeback and throws his arm over her shoulder.

"Ah, shit. I love this girl, Maverick. We needed another smartass."

"Hands off, fuckhead." He doesn't listen to me and starts walking with her to the door to exit the plane. He's damn lucky I like his twisted-up ass.

"You ready for this?" Pierce asks the minute we all step off the plane.

"More than ready. While you set it up, I'm going to call my mom." We walk straight to the office within the confines of our own compound. Jade squeezes my hand tightly, and I kiss her on her forehead before I let her go with them. I need to talk to my mom on my own.

Snagging my cell from the front pocket of my jeans, I slide the screen to find her name, then place the phone up to my ear while I hold my breath for her to answer.

"Hey, son." Her cheery voice instantly brings a smile to my face. "How's it going, mom?" I begin my pacing, back and forth in front of the office, my free hand running through my hair while I stress about what exactly to say. If I keep this shit up, I'll wear a path in the damn grass right here. I figure I may as well start with the most important thing.

"I met a woman. She's the one, mom." Her sharp, screeching scream has me pulling the phone away from my ear. It's followed by a string of curse words mixed with 'when can I meet her' and 'it's about damn time'.

"That's one of the reasons for my call. I thought you might want to come down here and stay a few days to meet her." It's partially the truth. I want nothing more than the two of them to meet. Under normal circumstances would be a hell of a lot better, but there isn't a damn thing normal about this. I want her here, even though she's protected where she is. My mind would feel better if she was here, with me, where I know for a fact she's safe. This compound is the safest place I know. I made sure we had the best of the best when we designed it.

"I can't, Kaleb. I have to work. You two should come here." I've been telling her for years to quit her job and let me take care of her, but the stubborn woman won't hear of it. There's no sense in trying to talk her into it. I should know, I get my stubbornness from her. When she makes up her mind about something, there is no changing it.

"You know how I feel about you working, mom, but I get it."

"First, I want to know why in the hell there is another man outside of my house. By the way, I should mention he's a very large, nice-looking man. Thanks for sending the nice-looking ones, Kaleb. Then tell me all about this woman who seems to have captured my son's heart."

I roll my eyes and spend the next half hour talking to her about anything and everything. I make sure to sidestep why she has extra security on her. She knows better than to ask. I make sure Amelie is ok, and we both stay silent for a moment toward the end. I know she has so many questions, and I love my mother for always respecting the fact I can't tell her everything.

We end our talk with me promising to bring Jade to her as soon as I can and her excitement about all the places she plans to take us when we do get to make the trip to see her. I have a feeling she's going to overwhelm Jade, but I know she can handle it. She knows my mother means the world to me, so she'll mean a lot to Jade for that very reason alone.

Keeping things from her makes me feel guilty as hell, but right now, I don't even know whether to tell her we killed her other son, or that I'm going to kill him. That doesn't really sound like a great conversation to have with your mother on any day, but definitely not the day she finds out you've met the woman of your dreams and that she is actually yours.

I see Jade peek through the curtain of the main cabin a few times to check on me as I finish up the call. How did I get so lucky to actually get the one woman who caught my eye to fall for me and prove herself to me over and over again?

I see her again and motion her outside to meet me. These tapes are going to be hard for me to watch, and I just hope I can control my anger when I do. Seeing what they saw will be hard, but I know this is something we need to do.

"You ok? Is your mom good?" she asks before she reaches me, and I reply instantly.

"She's good. I'm going to be alright once I get what's on these tapes behind me."

"I know you are. Come inside and let's face what we're up against. They have Pierce's footage ready to watch." I pull her back for a quick kiss, not because I can't keep my hands off of her this time, but because I want to feel her support before I go in to endure the disturbing mind-fuck I'm about to sit through.

"Jesus Christ, Jade," Pierce says. I know what he's talking about without even looking at him or without hearing the yelling. The gunshots on the screen showing she took off, leaving her position even though she was told to hold back. Shit, she was firing and killing every fucking thing that moved.

She shot them straight in the dick. I have to laugh out loud along with the rest of the guys. She's fucking crazy when it comes to this shit. And that makes me love her even more. I lean over to give her a kiss, not caring what the rest of them think. I don't keep my eyes from the screen long, waiting for the sight I'm here to see.

I continue to watch while my insides jump with every sound of a gunshot and every word spoken. My mind spins with pent-up frustration and anger the whole time the video plays. Harris even darted out of the woods right after Jade, both of them guns fucking blazing. I see Pierce and Jackson approaching from the other side, hear words flying like the wildfire emblazing my goddamn soul.

And then, fuck... there I am. Hanging helplessly on that damn tree. My head down. My body burned and bruised. I suck in a sharp breath when I see it's Harris who takes control over me. His large body covers some of the footage as he struggles and focuses on cutting my battered body down.

The sounds of him grunting and then watching him shield my body from the bullets slinging through the air pull deep inside my heart. I owe him my life. He'll get my thanks and will forever have my loyalty after what he did for me out there. I'll call him soon, but right now, I need to stay focused. I need to be sure my brother was among the dead. My eyes flit everywhere, while I search all the dead bodies to see if one of them is Ty.

I stand abruptly. Time ticks slowly as I try to count the endless bodies lying on the ground. My girl is solely focused on me, her lips pleading for me to look at her. To seek her out.

"Stop the damn tape," I yell loud enough to cause Jade to jump out of her seat and stand beside me.

"What is it? Did you see him?" Her hand grips my arm gently.

The tape stops rolling, but my gut doesn't. I know what I saw. It has to be him.

"Roll back about ten seconds, Pierce." I ignore Jade's plea beside me while the tape is moving backwards in slow motion then filtering to life again on the screen. "Brighten it. It's so fucking dark. There, on the roof. Enhance that," I say loudly. The screen pauses in an instant. My body stiffens. My heart explodes.

"Motherfucker," Pierce and Jackson both say at the same time.

"There he is. The fucker isn't dead," Jackson says with alarm.

"Is that him?" Jade points to the chicken shit sitting on the roof, his beady little eyes on the screen gazing back at me.

"Fuck. How the hell did we miss him? Our night vision should've picked that up." Kase stands along with the rest of them, knowing this is only the beginning.

"Goddamn it," I roar. I know my brother and that lopsided smirk on his face. The way he's gloating, he knows he's found my weakness. Ty isn't looking at the dead bodies on the ground. Not him, no, his eyes are on Jade, blazing with satisfied revenge.

"Yes. That's my fucking brother," I say to all of their backs as I stalk furiously out the door.

CHAPTER ELEVEN

JADE

I've made the call to my superior to let him know I've landed and my exact location. I've paced the floor while they set up. My heart clenched at the idea of watching that tape, and now I can't believe Kaleb just had to live through all of that a second time. I'm trained for shit like this and had to close my eyes a few times. Reliving his nightmare all over again is killing me. Listening to the sound of my voice when I saw him hanging there brought back all the fucked-up flashbacks of the reality of that night. It hurts me to watch him suffer like this.

I've followed him to his own cabin and refuse to let him isolate himself and relive this shit over and over. I told him I was in this with him, and I don't care if he's angry or not, I'm going in. I hear the slam of the bathroom door, so I try to open it, only to find he's locked it.

I've never seen him this angry and it scares me. I hope he won't do anything drastic without the rest of us, but I know he's going to try to shelter me from all of this.

"Kaleb. Please let me help." I lean my forehead against the door, not knowing what to say to get him to open it. I can hear him throwing up, and it's killing me to know his brother was that damn close, but I jumped the gun to save Kaleb. If I would've held strong like I was ordered to do, we could've scoped the area like we were supposed to and have the count before we went in. I wish I could say I wouldn't do the same thing again, but I would. I hope like hell I'm never put in the same type of situation again.

He's running the water now, and I'm relieved to hear he's no longer throwing up. I can hear him brushing his teeth and then just the sound of the water continues. He's gone silent.

"Kaleb. I told you to open this door. I'm here to help...." The door swings open and I stop yelling over the change in the air. He looks different. He's pasty with a strange look of uncontrollable fear on his face.

"You can't fucking help me. I need a few minutes to deal with this shit, and then I'll find you."

"I'm not leaving you." I stand firm. He's not forcing me out of this.

"Jade. I need a fucking minute. Goddammit. Give me a fucking minute. I wish like fuck I could go to the gym or go for a damn run, but right now, I'm trying to figure out how to deal with all of this aggression. You need to go, and I'll find you when I'm chilled the fuck out." He comes out of the bathroom and looks straight into my face, trying to intimidate me into leaving. I don't buy his move and won't play his games. I look into his eyes and let the same fear and determination stare right back at him. I'm not giving up on this, on him. I will not back down.

"I'm not fucking leaving. Work it out on me." He has aggression, and I can't think of a better way to work it out than to fuck me senseless. He's crazy if he thinks he needs a damn gym right now. There's no way he needs to be lifting weights. He can work around his wounds again; we did it today on the plane. We can do it again. I'm sure we can figure something out. Together.

"No." His response is steady and directly in front of my face.

"Why not?" I reply firmly, without flinching, even when he's trying to act like a fucking giant towering over me.

"Because I'm ready to fuck something up, Jade. I'm not going to take this out on you." His words are brittle, and I can see the chaos in his eyes.

"I can handle you, Kaleb. Please, don't shut me out. I just got you back." He looks at me closely, his eyes still filled with a desperation that worries me. He's seeking me out too.

"Jade. You don't know what you're asking for." He walks away from me toward the kitchen, leaving me to turn off the water he left running in the bathroom. I look around the room to see if there's any sign of what he was truly doing in here, but I see nothing broken, except the leftover shadows of his pent-up anger.

I look into the mirror and stop instantly when I see how tired I look. The last few weeks have been very trying, and it doesn't appear to get better anytime soon. I look worn and my features show how mentally and physically exhausted I am. I hear his footsteps coming back, but I don't move from the mirror. I just allow my eyes to meet his when he steps in behind me.

"I'm sorry. I'm just fucking livid that he knows about you now."

"We don't know that."

"Yes, we do. He'll come for you just to get to me."

"Then shouldn't you keep me close instead of pushing me away?" I watch his facial expression as he processes my words soften just slightly. He places a hand on the counter on each side of me, closing me in.

We both look into each other's eyes until he begins to talk. "He's a fucking monster, and now that he thinks I have something he needs, he'll be using all of his resources to get to me."

"So we go to him. We get your guys to locate him, then go finish the job." I won't let his brother destroy him. He's already done enough damage, and I'll be damned if I let him continue to tear him apart or hurt him anymore.

"You're fearless. And that scares the shit out of me." I'm not fearless, not when it comes to him. I'm scared out of my mind. I want a normal life with him. But we won't have it until Kaleb is free from this nightmare. I'm not going to tell him that. If I do, he'll shut me out completely.

"Kaleb. I've worked my entire career to become a soldier who can take on dangerous missions. The one thing they didn't prepare me for, is you. I'm not supposed to have the urge to break all the rules, but you've changed me. I want you. I want you safe. I want you happy. And I want you healthy. If anything interferes with that, I'm going to struggle keeping it low key, so I can stand by to watch. I won't apologize for going to you when I noticed they were about to piss on you. Those fuckers deserved to die, and I made it happen. Tell me you'd act any differently if it was me out there, and I'll call you a liar."

He finally smirks just slightly before he leans into my shoulder to kiss my neck.

"You're so fuckin' feisty and sexy. This badass is all mine. Fuck, I'm glad you're on my side." His hands move around to the front of my body, and he practically covers my entire torso with them. He slides two fingers between my legs over the top of my shorts, and I look into his eyes through the mirror. I'm not sure if my look is challenging him or encouraging him to continue, but he reads me loud and clear. His fingers drag my shirt up my stomach and then he slips his hand into the front of my shorts.

I welcome the change in his eyes and even open my legs wider for him to have better access.

"You really want me to take my aggression out on you?" I nod, giving him the response I hope he was looking for. He grabs a handful of my hair and pulls it tightly, forcing me to look into the mirror at him.

"I've been warning you about this, Jade."

I'm not sure if he's hoping to scare me away with his little threats, but I'm not going anywhere. I place my hand over his and push his finger, so that he's giving me more pressure against my clit. I know this will be my silent acceptance to his warnings, and I'm not disappointed when he takes his hand out abruptly before he becomes a complete alpha. He still has his hands wrapped in my hair, tugging it even tighter just before he pulls me into his chest, my face turned, so I can see his cheek before he speaks directly into my ear. "Clothes off. Now."

He releases my hair, and I watch him through the mirror as I slide each garment off in a slow, teasing way. I smile at him when he reaches between my legs to pinch my clit. "Bend over the sink. Watch your face while I take what's mine." I do what he says, but try to watch him instead. He's the one I want to see. He sees me searching for him and yanks my legs apart wider. "I said, look at your face, Jade. Watch how it changes when I pleasure you." I quickly obey as he slides two fingers into me. He bends to kiss my back, only to quickly stand again. "Fuck. I'm going to kill that motherfucker for fucking up my legs. I just want to taste you." I move without hesitation and climb onto my knees on the counter. He goes for my pussy instantly. His nibbles are perfect, and I love that he's not even being soft. His beard gives the perfect friction to my hungry nerves. I'm fully exposed to him and loving every move he makes.

He slips his thumb into my ass and two fingers into my pussy, moving them in and out while he talks to me.

"You see, I even thought of this right here." He continues to finger fuck me roughly, and I work to balance myself before he shoves me into the mirror. He grips my hair again, forcing me to look into his eyes.

"Tell me you thought of me behind you. Tell me you wanted me to fill you again just like I did in the desert." I nod very slowly, his tight grip only allowing me to move slightly. "Get down here. I want to watch your eyes in this mirror." I move my feet back down to the floor and spread them apart for him.

Watching him unzip his pants and start stroking his cock is the perfect tease for me. He works his hand up and down his length a few seconds and even hits his palm with it, sending a loud hammer sound through the room. *Shit, he's very hard and that was sexy as hell.* He smacks my ass with it before he starts to rub the tip over my entrance.

"Tell me, Jade. Do you want me in your ass? Or do you want it from behind?" I really don't care what he does as long as he fucks me.

"Just please, fuck me, Kaleb." He watches my face while he slides his cock into my pussy, slowly pulling my hair into a grip again. He forces my face forward, and I watch his eyes darken. He's in his element. I've never seen him sexier than he is right this very moment.

He slams into me hard, sending pain into my legs with each thrust. I take his aggression while he grips my hips and fucks me. He moves his hands over my breasts and grips them both to use for leverage to pull me into him with each thrust. When that isn't enough, he grabs my shoulders and drives into me harder and faster. My orgasm swarms all around me, but doesn't happen until he grips my throat, squeezing with enough force to cause my pussy to clench around his hard, massive cock. I welcome the rush over my body as he sends his heat deep into me with his final thrusts.

My legs are burning from the friction against the counter, but I don't dare move. I bask in the feeling of him deep inside me, while his cock twitches its way back to normal. We both breathe heavily in the mirror until he finally pulls out of me. I'm thoroughly fucked and immensely satisfied when he turns me around to face him. Without a word, he lifts me onto the countertop and kisses me like he'll never have the chance again. He's demanding my mouth to open wide while his tongue invades. Taking and tasting and delivering a quench to the thirst I've felt since we first left for Mexico. If he keeps this up, I'll be squirming to have him between my legs every moment of the day.

I missed this man, and I'm so relieved I get to have this with him after I thought it was over. After seeing him in the hospital bed so weak and confused then torn up inside, while he sheltered his feelings of hurt and anger from everyone.

I love Kaleb Maverick whether he's soft, sweet, hard, or demanding. He's mine, and I'll kill his brother if given the chance for even thinking of trying to take him away from me.

"You feel like a shower?" He speaks against my cheek as he pulls away. I nod and let him carry me the few feet to his large shower. He was correct in saying he would fuck me until we both couldn't walk. My legs will be bruised from his force, but he seems to be walking fine. Next time, I may have to remedy that.

He cherishes me like the soft Kaleb I know while we're in the shower. I can tell by his touch he's trying to appreciate every inch of my skin. He's in deep thought, so I just let him slide his hands over my wet body as he chooses. He's such a complex man, and it prides me to know somehow, some way, I am the woman he chose to consume. I can't even remember how boring my life was without him.

The water begins to get cold before he finishes. He turns it off and slides two towels in from around the glass door. He still hasn't said a word when we both step out onto the rug.

His perfect body is on display for me, and I don't waste time not appreciating it. He watches me as I wrap my towel around my chest, then wraps his own around his waist. His hand brushes my ass when he walks by to leave me to get ready. Before he passes, he turns my face to him for a kiss. This one is slow and understanding. Like we've made it through the angry aggression and now we both realize we're here for each other.

"I'm going to call my parents and Mallory while I'm making us something to eat." I focus on drying my hair with my towel. The steam is billowing out of the bathroom behind us after I take a few steps into his bedroom.

"You do that. I'm going to check in with the guys and see if we can get a plan started. I want this over with. I can't live my damn life outside of here, not knowing what his next move is going to be. We need to find him and strike first. This time, he's not escaping." With all the numerous emotions scouring through the both of us right now, I'm glad he's going to check in with the guys. They need to know he's doing alright. They've driven down this road of mass destruction right along with both of us, their anger and fear bleeding as much as ours.

"I love you," I say tenderly, the words sweetly escaping like I want them to. Even though he's not going to be that far away from me and we're all safe here, I still hate the fact I can't watch over him and be there to help him if he loses his shit again. I'm not an idiot. I know damn well he's going to study that tape and repeat every line and angle of it over and over until he's satisfied he hasn't missed a thing. If he needs this, I'll give it to him, but I'll be right here if he needs me.

"Love you too, babe. And Jade," he says with adoration, "you're incredible, and I'm so fucking lucky to have you." I stand there with my towel wrapped around me, my hands going to my throat, to the same spot his hand was encircling not even a half hour ago.

"So am I, Kaleb," I whisper to the closed door.

I make my way to the kitchen to find something for dinner and make a phone call I won't miss making again.

"Hey, mom." I can't help but flash a smile into the airy kitchen when she hollers through the phone for my dad to pick up the other line without even acknowledging me.

"Jade, honey," she finally says. "Well, hello there, baby girl." My dad bellows out, and I sit my cell on the long island countertop in Kaleb's kitchen. I start filtering through the fridge for something quick and easy to make while I listen to my parents go back and forth a few more times about if they can hear each other.

It amazes me that this damn place is stocked with fresh fruit and vegetables. Hell, there's even juice, milk, a variety of meats, and beer. Of course, there would be beer. God knows a man like Kaleb would have it nearby.

"What have you two been up to?" My dad laughs loudly, and I almost drop the tomato and head of lettuce on the floor. I've decided on BLTs. "What's so funny?" I ask. I sit the items on the counter, then reach in and grab the bacon. I kick the door shut with my foot and place the bacon alongside the other items before I set out in search of a skillet.

"Our lives are boring. We've been doing the same routine for years, baby girl. Now, tell me what you can. Are you doing okay?" Ha. I wish I could tell them the truth, that I've been suffering like I never imagined possible. That the man I love has been all but dying a slow death inside, because he can't wrap his head around his own brother beating him half to death before leaving him to hang for the wild animals to feed off of. Instead, I go with my heart.

"I'm in love," I say tentatively, starting up the gas stove as I go to warm the skillet.

"Come again?" My dad seems to be doing all the talking, while my mother's heavy breathing and gasping 'oh my god's' swelter through the phone.

"His name is Kaleb. He's retired from the Army. Owns his own private security firm." That's all the information I'm going to give them for now. They don't need to know how we met. To be honest, I have no clue if I can tell them or not. My mind is beyond foggy to remember a damn thing right now.

"Well, shit. I'm dying to meet him. I'll need to see with my own eyes if he's good enough for my daughter." I laugh at my dad's joke. He's the basic nobody's-ever-going-to-be-good-enough-for-my-daughter kind of dad.

"This makes my heart swell, sweetheart. I can't wait to meet him. And don't pay your dad any attention. It won't matter if you marry the man and have a handful of babies. No one will ever be good enough for you in his eyes." Oh, good god. Marriage and babies. "Shit. Mom. Marriage isn't even in the picture."

This joking banter between the three of us is exactly what I need. I'm laughing and carrying on with my parents for the longest time, and it feels as if no time has passed by us at all. I'm more comfortable than when I showed up unannounced at their hours several weeks ago.

We say our goodbyes, then I try a few times to get a hold of Mallory, but it goes to voicemail every damn time. I leave one last message for her to call me back while my mind wonders where the heck she is. She knows I had to take off, but we both talked about getting together once I returned. It's not like her to ignore my calls.

"Where are you, Mallory?" I ask out loud like she can hear me.

CHAPTER TWELVE

KALEB

I sit on the front porch and listen to Jade talk to her parents. The sound of her laughter coming from my kitchen brings a much-needed smile to my face. I'm so glad she has a great relationship with them now. It's something that's important to me, so I need it to be important to the person I chose to be with forever.

Someone up above must be paying a bit of attention to know that hearing her flit around my house, banging the cupboards, and the sweet sound of her voice is a necessity for me right now.

She's everything to me. The way she pushed me to take out my anger on her in a much-needed fuck, no less than broke me. I love nothing more than to fuck her sweet body and pound us both into a stupor. And I will many times in my life, but never again when my mind is out of control. When I feel like I'm going out of my goddamn mind with worry and fear over where the fuck Ty is and what the hell he has planned.

He's coming. I can feel it to the deepest part of my bones. There was a warning in his eyes that shot straight to my heart. He fucking knows about her; I damn well know he does.

The idea of letting her out of my sight even for just a blink of an eye sends a chill down my spine so deep it frightens the hell out of me. And I'm a man who isn't afraid of anyone or anything, but him. I can't even comprehend what he would do to her if given the chance. She's staying right here. I'll tie her up and leave Harris behind if I have to. There's no way in hell she's going on this personal mission with me. I won't take a chance when it comes to her.

Speaking of Harris, I need to call him. What I need to talk to him about should be said in person, but being that he's not here, a phone call will have to do.

I push myself up from the wooden steps and snatch my phone from my pocket. I find his name in my contacts and slowly make my way toward the office as it begins to ring.

"Maverick," Harris answers on the second ring.

"You make it back to the ranch or you still climbing out of the pile of shit the Army has you in?" He laughs loudly on the other end, and a slight smirk spreads across my face.

"No shit slinging here, dude. Paperwork up the ass though. All of you make it to the compound okay?" He sounds out of breath, and I wonder if he's working out. Lucky fucker. I'd give anything to be able to pump some damn iron right now.

"Yeah. We're here." I pause.

"You good, man? If you are, I'll file that paperwork for my medal." He laughs.

He might be joking about the medal. However, I couldn't agree more. He deserves more than my simple thank you for taking it upon himself to stay with her in Mexico. Jade told me how he told her he was there for her, just to make sure she went nowhere alone.

"I'm getting there. As far as saving my ass, that's one of the reasons why I'm calling. We saw the tapes. I know what you did. You put your life before mine, man. I'll never forget that." At the time it all happened, I couldn't comprehend anything around me except her voice. I had no idea who was with her.

I can almost hear the cocky smirk that I know spreads across his face. Even though his next words are like a surprise uppercut to my jaw. I know he means them.

"You'd do the same for me." Damn right, I would.

"Just don't go looking for trouble so I have to." Before he can reply, I hear a female hollering his name in the background.

"Is that Mallory?" I ask suspiciously.

"Yeah. I'm at their place. The ranch will have to wait a while. It's back to the grind for me. You mentioned another reason for calling." His voice is hesitant.

"He's alive," I say, knowing damn well I don't have to say more. "Keep an eye on Mallory. You got me?" I run my free hand down my face. The tension building across my neck and shoulders is growing the more I think about all the people we need to protect.

"You let me know the plan and I'm there, Kaleb." I should have known he would be willing to battle and take down the fucking devil himself. The last thing I say to him before I hang up is, "You know I will."

Tucking my phone back into my pocket, I make my way back to the office. Pierce is just hanging up the phone, and Jackson is sitting on top of the desk with a beer in his hand, staring blankly out the window.

"Fuck, man. You alright?" Both of them stand. Jackson walks to the small fridge and grabs a beer, handing it to me before I even have the chance to sit down. I unscrew the cap and damn it, the cold, refreshing brew feels good as I tip the bottle and chug a good half of it down.

"No." There isn't anything remotely alright about any of this, except for the fact everyone I care about is safe for now.

"Go home. We can start fresh in the morning. Kase and Steele will be here early." Pierce wants me to rest. He should know me better than that. I can't rest when I know what's coming in one way, shape, or form.

"The President wants to meet with you and Kase tomorrow on conference. We've been instructed to only allow the two of you in the room for security purposes." I look up from my beer to see him reading an email.

"Wonder what that's about? Kase did brief him after the mission, right?"

"Yes, he did. In fact, I sat in on that call with him on the plane while taking you to the hospital. He wanted instant information on you, and that was as quick as we could get to him."

"Has he said anything about Al-Quaren?"

"We don't have any details. Just know that he's been interrogated heavily." Jackson slides off the desk and grabs another handful of beers to hand out. I take down the last of mine and gladly take the other one off his hands.

"Damn, I needed this beer today."

"Well, I'm not going to worry about what he's going to say. We went in and did our job. We never asked for their help in going back in, so as far as he's concerned, it should be a great mission accomplished." Pierce begins to walk a small path as he paces along two walls before he begins to talk again. "We should just plan to meet after that conference call to decide our next plan of action. We have to go after Ty. I can pull a few strings to see if we can get some more information on his ring before we just blindly go in."

"I agree. Until then, we can get an update on Juice and Drew. Have you heard from them since they left for their mission?"

"Yes. Their teams are headed back. Juice said if we need them, they're ready for the call. They're taking a break from shit until then though."

"I don't blame them." They've been on that mission for over a month now. Hell, that's longer than I've known Jade. I'm thankful I didn't go on that one myself. I shake my head at everything I would've missed. Yes, I would've missed Mexico, but I would've missed Jade. In the end, we're together, so I'd never think back on any of the shit we've been through. My only worry is the future.

"You know, I'm due a fucking vacation myself. I'm supposed to take Jade to Bali. I figure I'd better work on that once we get shit calmed down here and my brother handled."

"You lucky bastard. Just be glad you got to her first." Jackson stops listening and decides to join our conversation.

"You wouldn't have had a chance in hell." I take another long swig of my beer and watch Jackson smile. We both know he's just rousing me. I'm not going to let it work today. Jade and I have been through far too much for me to get butt hurt when Jackson runs his mouth.

"You're probably right, but I would've had fun trying." His loud laughter fills the room, and I can't help but smile at his easiness. This guy rarely gets stressed and just takes shit as it comes. "She fucking loves you though. Shit. I thought for a second we were all going down in that helicopter when she pointed that rifle at Harris' temple."

"She what?" I almost choke on my drink and look to him to continue.

"Hell, Pierce. Play his ass that section of her recordings. That shit will haunt me till the day I die. When I get a woman to react about me like she did to you, then I'll know I've met the one." Pierce stands and quickly clicks a few times on the computer before her voice is echoing through the speakers. My skin crawls, remembering the same words I could hear in my headgear, but it quickly runs past that point and her rationale is gone. I shake my head as I listen to her demand they go back.

"Shit. She was pissed. I'm surprised nobody got their ass shot." The recording continues, and I hear her threaten Harris. I can feel how hysterical she was, and I know she felt completely alone. Fuck, I'm glad that wasn't me on that chopper and Harris on the ground, because I know damn well she would've reacted to either of us like that. Of course, minus the whole love thing.

I can't say another word about Harris. At this point, he's proven himself to be a great ally, and I love knowing that if something does happen to me, he will take care of Jade for me. I also know he has enough respect for me to know his place.

I hear him tell her he's there for her wherever they're going. "Alright. Stop it. I can't take that shit again." Jackson stands once more, handing me a third beer. I take it, knowing it'll be my last for the night. I know Jade is working on dinner and honestly, nothing sounds better after what I just heard than having a normal night with the woman I love, and from the sounds of the insanity on the tape... she deeply loves me too.

I take my time on the short walk back to my cabin. It's just the perfect distance from the main house. I have my privacy, yet I'm near the team when we need to be ready to work.

"It smells great. How'd you know I love bacon?" I walk into my cabin with the air filled with the smell of bacon cooking. This might be one of the sexiest things I've seen her do.

"Just a guess with the three packages in there. Figured a quick sandwich tonight, then I'm thinking tomorrow, I'd like to go meet your mom." I watch a smile cross her face and kiss her grinning lips quickly before she continues talking. "Then you can meet my parents. I figure if we're doing these missions like this and professing our love to each other all the time... we should know each other's family a little."

"I like that idea. But only if we talk about Bali on the road." I do want to meet her parents and even her brothers.

"Deal. Sit and I'll make you a plate."

"I have to meet Kase in the morning. He's coming in, and the President wants to talk to just the two of us." She looks instantly concerned, and I regret telling her anything at all.

"What do you think he wants?"

"Not sure. But I'll know in the morning." She sits down beside me, and I watch her face fill with even more worry.

"What if he wants us to go back?" I want to tell her they'll be no us in that formula, but I know not to go there till it's time. She'll lose her shit if that does go down.

"Then we go." I've already decided I'd go and find my brother in the process. If I can pull off another mission for my country, then I'll sure as hell be in. "You're sexy as fuck when you start thinking."

"Kaleb. This is serious. I don't know if you're ready to be back in full force." I stand instantly, lifting my plate as I do.

"I can't deal with this handicapped Kaleb shit. I'm still functional and would never put my team in danger if I thought I couldn't do it all. Besides, we don't even know what he wants yet." I make myself sit back down. Shit, my emotions are out of control. I need to get a damn grip.

"I never said you were handicapped. And I know how protective you are, but so am I, Kaleb. You were tortured out there, and you need to take a break from this shit for a few weeks." I can't make her that promise until I know my brother is taken care of.

"I will when I get Ty. I can't until then." She looks down at her plate and starts to think about something. I don't ask her because honestly, I hate the tension between us right now.

"I heard you held a rifle to Harris's temple."

"I did," she says matter-of-factly without an ounce of regret. "I was losing my fucking mind and can't apologize for wishing we'd have dropped back down and fought for you."

"Jade, stop. They did everything right. On a mission, we have to do what's required to bring in the subject if that's the given mission. There were so many of them hiding, we would've lost men for sure if you had dropped back down."

"Yeah. Well, at the time, it seemed like the logical thing to do. I don't leave anyone behind. Period. And I hope one day they don't have the same hell thrown on them if we have to leave off without them."

"I agree." I take a few bites while she just watches me like she has more to say, but doesn't.

She's angry and I get it. I would be if I were her. Hell, I'd be a lying motherfucker if I didn't admit that fear is desperately trying to ease its way into my veins. The only thing stopping it from breaking through is my anger. There isn't a damn thing that's going to break that barrier down until I make sure Ty's good and dead from every goddamn bit of pain he has brought to my world. He'll be unrecognizable by the time I'm done with him. Mark my words. That is a promise I intend to keep.

I know better than anyone that my body is far from healed or ready to head out, let alone lead a mission. But fuck it, this is my job, and if my intuition is correct, I know whoever or whatever we are after is going to help lead us to Ty. Right now, though, I need to sleep, preferably naked and with my sexy as fuck, blond woman snuggled close to my side.

"I'm going to get ready for bed," Jade speaks from the kitchen, where she's just finished cleaning up. She let me work while she took care of it tonight. That's not something I expect from her, but I love that she knew I needed a moment today. I have a few things I need to do. I've been sitting here the last few minutes, thinking about all this while texting back and forth with my sister for us to surprise my mom tomorrow. It's been awhile since I've seen them. With everything that's happened, I need to hug both of them. I need to see with my own damn eyes they're alright.

Like I said before, my mom can pick up on every damn thing. She'll know the minute I walk through her front door that I'm hurt. Then she'll ride my ass about quitting, or guarding some dull-ass politician, or becoming someone's personal bodyguard. No fucking way. I was born for this shit. I serve and protect my country, and in some cases have to go in and kill the enemy.

Jade went on a little terror scare about the possibility of me heading back out. I let her bitch up a storm then told her enough. We'll deal with whatever is thrown our way, and we'll deal with it together. That shut her up for about five seconds. Goddamn woman is the most stubborn person I have met.

"I'm coming." I stretch my arms above my head, my muscles pulling tight. The first thing I'm gonna do tomorrow morning when I wake is work out. It fucking sucks that I have to start out with half the weight I was using before. It's going to feel like I'm lifting a brown paper bag instead of what I'm used to.

I close down my laptop. I've been studying the area where the crazy-ass fucker came close to killing me. I remember him saying he had a home back in the woods somewhere. I remember him calling it his kingdom, or was it his domain?

"I'll find you, Ty, and when I do, you're going to be praying to the devil to take your fucking soul."

I lock up the house, grab the charger to my phone, and make my way to my bedroom before I fall to my knees. Jade's already in bed.

The sight of her in my bed has my cock coming to life. If I didn't notice how exhausted she was when we were having dinner, I'd flip her ass over and make love to her nice and slow. But she needs a good night's sleep. She hasn't slept in a bed since before we left, because she was at my side the entire time

I was in the hospital. She either slept in the recliner or next to me once I was able to succumb to the pain of having her that close to my body.

"You're beautiful," I tell her. My skin itches to be close to her, and I want to hold her and feel her warm body up against mine.

"I'd be even more beautiful in your arms." Good choice of words, baby. I strip out of my clothes. Her gaze travels down to my rock hard cock. I quirk a brow and she smiles.

"Yeah. One look and you have me hard." It's the truth.

I twist my body around to shut off the light, never taking my eyes off of her. Once I make it to my bed, I welcome her sliding her ass as close to me as she can get. My cock jumps at the feel of her as it rests in the curve of her tight little ass.

"Go to sleep, baby." My arm rests just below the swell of her breasts, and my face is buried against her neck and into her hair.

"Kaleb."

"Yeah." My eyelids are heavy as I answer.

"I love you."

"I love you too, Mrs. Maverick." That seems to get a chuckle out of us both.

"About that," she whispers.

"It's ok. Just go to sleep, Jade." *Someday*, I think to myself before I fall into a deep sleep, where I dream of her instead of succumbing to the nightmares of the torture I've endured that have been tormenting my troubled mind.

CHAPTER THIRTEEN

JADE

I've been sitting on the porch for over an hour, watching the door to the office I watched Kaleb disappear behind.

Our bags are in the back of the SUV and I'm ready to go.

We slept for nine hours straight last night. I don't think I moved the entire time. I would have kept on sleeping if he hadn't had to get up and work out, and then rush out the door to have his so-called private meeting with Kase and the President.

Now I sit here, worried out of my ever-loving mind. I'm about to unglue my ass from these steps and bust in there. My gut tells me that whatever the hell is going down in there, I'm not going to be a part of, and that pisses me the fuck off.

Kaleb wants to protect me, and I love him even more for that. But, damn it, can't he see I want to protect him too? That the thought of him going somewhere without me, especially when he isn't in the right state of mind, not to mention he isn't healed, is tearing me apart?

What pisses me off even more is my hands are tied. If these orders come from the President, there isn't a damn thing I can do.

I'm startled when my phone rings beside me. I glance down, wondering who the hell would be calling at eight o'clock in the morning. I fumble, picking it up when I see Mal's name flashing on the screen.

"Where have you been?" I say sarcastically. I've been worried about her. Worry seems to be all I've been doing lately. I'm sick and tired of it. I want normal. Whatever the hell that might be.

"Hello to you too." The sound of her voice alone pulls a beaming grin across my face.

Then, like I've been hit over the head with a two by four, it dawns on me and slaps me in the face. I haven't heard a word from Harris either. That's unlike him, not to check in with me. They're together. I know they are.

"What you been doing, Mallory? Or should I say, who?" I laugh, my over-active temper subsiding because it's my best friend on the other end of this line.

"Ah. Jade Elliott. The clever smartass is back. Welcome home. I missed you." Yeah, right. I bet she did up until she hooked up with Harris.

"So. Harris, huh?" I stand, my ass is numb from sitting here.

"Yeah. He called me. God, Jade, he is one hell of a..."

"Stop. I don't want to know." I'm not about to tell her I know. Well, technically, I don't. But still, I'm not telling her a thing. Especially when she keeps going on about how sweet he is to her. I listen as she carries on for our entire conversation about him. How he left for the base an hour or so ago but promised to call her as soon as he could.

I'm happy for her, I really am. I know Mallory though. Sometimes better than she knows herself. I'm not about to burst her bubble with my worry. Mallory isn't cut out to date a man who has to leave at the drop of a hat to go fight for his country, ready to sacrifice his life. She's a wonderful person and the best friend anyone could ask for, and she may have a mouth on her with no filter, who tells you like it is, but Mallory worries more than anyone I know.

The door swings open, finally. I smile wide when I see the look on all the guys' faces as they walk out one by one.

"Hey, Mal. The guys are walking toward me. We're heading home. I should be back in a few days."

"I can't wait to see you," she returns.

"Ask Harris if he wants to come over to my parents' for dinner Saturday night." It's crazy how this past month or so has gone. Meeting Kaleb like I did. Then falling in love with him. When I told him last night about the conversation with my parents and how my mom talked my dad into having a big get-together, he honestly seemed to be looking forward to something for the first time since this entire mission went to shit.

This demanding and bossy man has a loyalty to family. I've known it all along with the way he talks freely about his mother and sister, not to mention the overflowing love he has for all these guys. Underneath his hard shield is a man who's not afraid to show how much others mean to him. It's one of the many reasons why I love him. It's also one of the reasons why I'm worried. He may be hiding how he truly feels about his brother. A big part of him does hate Ty, but—and it's a huge but—no matter what he tries to tell anyone, I know it's killing him slowly inside to deal with this shit.

"Dad's barbeque chicken. Hell, yes, I'll be there whether he can be or not. Love you," she says quickly, and I tell her the same before I hang up while watching what feels like a dozen pair of eyes trained on me. Every set of them screams power and determination. They are also warning me to not ask a damn thing.

"You ready?" Kaleb lifts me off my feet and plants a hard, closed-mouth kiss to my lips.

"No. Not until you guys tell me what the hell is going on?" It's Jackson who gets my hard glare after Kaleb puts me down again on solid ground. A ground that feels like it's trying to suck me in. These assholes are keeping something from me, and I don't like it.

"Jade." Kaleb says my name like a warning. I keep my eyes on Jackson. His smirk is pissing me off. This is not the time for him to act like an asshole. He's itching to give me some smart-ass retort, that's why I'm glaring at him like I want to kick him square in his damn dick.

"What's going on?" I demand.

"Baby. I'll tell you later. Right now, I want to forget all of this shit for a few days and spend some time with our families." Even though the sun is shining down on us and the humidity in the air is letting me know it's going to be a sweltering hot day, a cold shiver runs up and down my spine. Goosebumps caress my skin. Whatever it is, it's bad, very bad.

"We need to go or we'll miss our flight." I internally take note of all their faces. Analyzing is what I do best, and these assholes know that.

"You're lucky you found her first, dickhead." Jackson leans down and plants a kiss on my cheek, pulling me in close for a hug as he begins to whisper into my ear. "Cheer up, buttercup. I promise to protect that big ape of yours. You have nothing to worry about. Just relax." I squeeze him tight, knowing it's bothering him to keep whatever this is from me. It should be Kaleb with the guilty conscience.

If it's no big deal, then fucking tell me. I almost force those words out of my mouth. I know better though. I leash it all in and just observe and watch every single one of them. They can't look me in the face when they tell me goodbye. These fuckers are terrible at this shit.

They think I don't know they're all hiding something, and I've had it with all of them. I'll keep my shit together and enjoy my day meeting the two women in Kaleb's life who mean everything to him. But I can promise one thing... before that, I'll work on Kaleb. This could be a very long flight.

*****

The flight so far has been awkward. Neither of us tried to hide that there's an issue suffocating us both.

"You acting all pissy and shit makes my dick hard." I mull over my response before answering him. Does he really want to go there right now?

"It's just like you to try to deflect my attention and avoid the issue, Kaleb." I sneer, and he smirks. I'm beyond pissed. I'm fucking livid. How dare he keep a damn thing from me. Especially with everything we've been through. I know I'm making this about me. This is about how I'm going to be able to handle the shit that has been dealt this time. About how I'm going to feel if he travels out there somewhere without me, which is very likely to happen.

"I hear the clicking noises going off in your pretty little head, Jade. If you really need to know, it's nothing. A small job; one I've done many times. We'll be in and out and back home within a day." Kaleb is lying to me. He shifted in his seat, which isn't like him at all. That right there, along with him not being able to make eye contact, is one of the first signs I look for when interrogating someone to see if they're lying.

He's a pro at this job. Very rarely does he make a mistake. So why is he lying to me? I guess I should be happy he can't be the expert he's trained to be when it comes to lying to me. But I'm not. I will get to the bottom of this one way or another.

"Fine, Kaleb," I concede. I'm not in the mood to argue, not here anyway. Not when we're about to land and head straight to his mom's house.

How I wish I had time to call my superior right now. I still have a few weeks left of my extended leave. Maybe I should schedule a meeting and talk to him about my request to be assigned to work with Kaleb on all of his missions. This way, there wouldn't be a damn thing Kaleb could do or hide from me.

I may need to reconsider that thought, if this is how he's going to treat me. Did he forget that quickly that I was the one who saved his ass in Afghanistan? I tried like hell to save him in Mexico and forced his team to rush his rescue. Why would he even consider keeping me away from any of his missions?

With those so-called clicking noises in my head, I start to think about what I'm going to do about this. I've fought my entire career to be treated equal, and he seemed to be the first man to give me that respect right off the bat. Now, he's retracting all of that and acting like I'm a piece of fucking glass that can't handle any real pressure. What he doesn't realize is I now have this need to protect him, when I'm sure he thinks he's doing the same for me. I'll be damned if he's going to treat me like a fragile woman.

The plane ride was irritably quiet after our brief disagreement. He dozed for a bit, while I watched his handsome features. He looks so peaceful with his eyes closed, and yet I know there is a major storm brewing in his head. The eye of it is about to hit. I can feel it. That's the only reason why I backed down from the real shit I'm feeling inside.

Kaleb may have gotten the impression I receded because he told me to, but I'm just calculating how to go about this. He's a complicated man, who is as stubborn as anyone I've ever met. He knows I'm his real challenge, but I refuse to let it darken the day I meet his mom and sister. I'll talk to him as soon as we leave their house.

I try really hard to set it all to the back of my mind, but I'm still fuming by the time we walk through the terminal and even down the stairs toward baggage claim, where we meet Kaleb's mom and sister. It all temporarily subsides the moment I see the female with a mile-wide smile on her face once she spots her son.

"Kaleb." She wraps both her arms around his waist in a hug one can only get from their mother. It's a sight to behold, seeing this big, bearded man covered in tats with muscles bulging in his shirt sleeves squeeze his mom while she rests her head on his chest.

"I missed you, old lady." I haven't given a whole lot of thought on what to expect when I met his family, but surely not this. I feel like a damn intruder as I watch her pull away from him only long enough to look at his face through her tears, then go in for another tight hug.

"You must be Jade." I turn to a woman I assume is his sister when I hear my name called. They look nothing alike, except those same deep, penetrating eyes. She's free and clear of makeup and absolutely stunning.

"It's nice to finally meet you, Amelie," I express truthfully as my hand goes out to shake hers.

"A true soldier, I see." She takes my hand in hers. She seems very warm and friendly, and that's something I'm not accustomed to.

"You have no idea how happy we are to finally meet the woman who has captured Mr. Grouchy Pants here." She punches her brother in his arm, obviously to get his attention. I love reconnecting moments like this, especially now with everything this tender-hearted yet struggling man has been through.

I feel the love pouring out of his mom when the two switch positions, allowing Amelie and Kaleb to embrace. He keeps his arm around her neck and pulls me into the other side of his body.

"Mom. This is Jade. Jade, my mom, Evie." No handshake from her. I'm brought into her embrace as well and have no choice but to encircle her in my own arms. *She reminds me of my mom.*

"This is a great day. Finally, he has found someone. I hope he treats you right." Evie teases her son as she steps back from me. Her gaze goes back and forth between the two of us, and I know she's observing us and probably picking up on a little tension even though we're both trying to hide it.

"Of course, I do. I had to live with the two of you, didn't I? Specifically, this one." He jeers his head toward his sister.

"Ha. Come on, Jade. Let me fill you in on the younger days of the badass, pain in the ass Kaleb Maverick." Amelie hooks her arms through mine. Her loud voice carries us all the way through the airport until we're outside and in the car. Her laughter and stories continue until we're about halfway to his mom's house. I love hearing her insight and smile even wider when Kaleb corrects her story to his view of how it went.

We pull into the long drive, and I can't take my eyes off the house in front of me. Its historical beauty takes my breath away. "This is gorgeous," I tell them as Kaleb grabs ours bags and leads me through the black rod iron fence. There's a swinging gate to the white picket fence and green painted stairs that match the color of the house.

"Wait until you see the inside." Amelie opens the big, wooden door, and as we step through it, I let out an unfamiliar gasp. I don't gasp when it comes to material things. I don't get all tied up in knots over homes, but this.... Seeing where Kaleb grew up, pictures of him and his sister and Ty in every stage of their lives all over the walls and along the mantel of the fireplace, brings tears to my eyes.

How could Ty turn his back on this? How could he walk away from a family who's full of support and unconditional love? I could ask myself the same question about the few years I became detached from my family. Although, I lost my true self when I lost my brother. My heart bleeds for his mom, his sister, and for him. Because, as of now, Ty is very much alive in this family.

CHAPTER FOURTEEN

KALEB

As much as I've enjoyed the interaction with all of my girls today, seeing my mom's face light up when she saw me and met Jade was the highlight. My fucking body is tired. I've hidden it well from everyone but Jade. Every damn time I moved, her head snapped in my direction, watching my every move. She's on to me about many things, but I'll have to let her fuss over me when it comes to my recovery. It's about time to go.

Jade and I have two days before we head over to her parents. I intend to use those days fully. Fucking her sweet body before I drop the bomb that's sure as fuck going to explode in my face.

We leave Sunday morning to head back to Mexico. Al-Quaren finally talked; in fact, he squealed and ratted out the name of one of the most infamous Mexican fugitives on the FBI most wanted list: Fernando Sanchez. Hell, I knew the second I heard his name that he's behind so much more than just drug trafficking. I remember seeing his name when we were working on the job to put an end to the sex trade ring that was discovered.

The informant for that mission mentioned an American man. I've never even considered that my brother could be that disgusting filth we investigated and were never able to uncover his identity. Whoever he was seemed to always stay just one step ahead of us on that mission. It was the reason we relocated the entire team to the compound. We needed high-end security and completely secure facilities to meet in. Our homes were no longer safe to plan missions of that magnitude. Hell, we even began to think one of our own was feeding information to the damn enemy.

Once we intercepted the delivery of over one hundred teenage girls, we actually killed three of the leaders in that ring and handed over files on countless international leaders trying to purchase the young girls.

It makes vomit rise in my stomach to think my brother may be the 'American' they kept referring to. I continue to watch my mom prepare her coffee pot so that it's ready and waiting for her when she wakes up at five in the morning like clockwork.

"Kaleb. What are you hiding from me?" I lean against the counter, knowing I'll hate this conversation.

"You know I can't talk to you, mom." I bow my head in frustration.

"Why do I think there's at least something you can say?" She turns to face me and stares at me with soft eyes, her look saying so much to me, and I struggle to find a way to make her relax about this whole situation

"Not sure. Just let me do my job and do what the security guys say."

"You gonna tell me why you've tripled the guys out there?"

"I'm working on a very dangerous project and won't risk your safety. Or Amelie's. It's just a precautionary step and I need you to cooperate with them at all times, mom." There's no way I can tell her I'm protecting her from the chance her own son could use her against me to draw information about an international terrorist. Jade walks in, distracting us both from any further conversation.

"Don't be gone so long this time, son." My mom places a kiss on my cheek and moves to Jade, where she embraces her tightly. I'll admit, today tugged on my heart, seeing all three of these women interact with each other. The happiness gleamed from my mom's eyes, because all she's ever wanted was for her children to find someone who loved them and be happy. She knows I've found it with Jade. She knew it when I talked on the phone about her. That's something I've never done with any of my other relationships. With all the questions she's slung at Jade today, I suspect she knows why I've fallen for her.

I've put on a damn good act for everyone today. Thank Christ for that. If she knew how fucked up my body was or the shit I've been through, that spark would die out of her. No goddamn way will I do anything to bring her any more pain. I'm barely containing the pain inside of me myself. It's mainly emotional pain at this point, but I'm beginning to think that may be worse than anything physical. Now, I'm just ready to go home and crawl inside my woman to forget everything that's stressing me the hell out.

"Next week, mom," I respond then lift my chin at Amelie, who's on her phone, standing on the porch.

I slide into my Jeep next to Jade, who's buckling up her seatbelt. "Thanks for picking her up for me." I give my thanks once again to the two of them for going and getting my ride for me. I crank the engine and god, does she purr like the sweet little machine she is.

"You can cut the acting now that we're alone." Jade's angry voice detonates through the small confinement of my Jeep as I pull away from the house.

"Not acting with you. It was all for them and you know it. Am I hurting? Fuck, yes, I am. My back is killing me." I decide to let her know exactly where I'm hurting before she has the chance to ask.

"No pain anywhere else?" Her wide eyes stare at me suspiciously from the passenger seat. She's not only talking about my physical pain here, she's digging. I can tell she wants to know if I'm in pain or feeling guilty about lying to her today.

I knew the minute I fucked up on that plane by barely being able to choke out a damn lie. Funny how you can hide all signs of lying to everyone else in your life, but when it comes to the one person you care about the most, all sense of ability flies out the goddamn window.

"My cock," I say sarcastically, hoping like hell it will put her in a better mood. I get why she's all uptight, but she can cut her act as well. If she's pissed, then fucking tell me.

I need her feisty attitude, her out-of-control mouth, and I need her to say what's on her mind. Not hold it in. Granted, we haven't been alone for her to challenge me in the way I know she wants to, but fuck, I'm all ears now.

Then I need her support on this when I lay the bombshell out on the table. She won't agree to stay behind, so I can't share the details with her. This situation is more dangerous than I thought. I'm damn lucky to even be breathing her in for the next few days before I face the insanity. Jade is not the one in charge here. I am when it comes to this shit, and she is not fucking going on this mission. She is staying here where I know she's safe. I'll haul her sexy ass to the compound and tie her ass up if I have to.

"You tell me what the hell is going on, and I'll relieve the pain in your cock." There she is. The one I've fallen for. The smart-mouthed woman who's been holding back her hostility and anger all damn day.

"I told you all I can, Jade." She exhales deeply, and I wait for it. Her spark is building and her anger is igniting while all I have to say is... bring it on. May as well get this shit done now, because the minute we step through the door of her apartment, I'm feasting on her. I'll fuck her with my mouth until she screams, then I'll turn around and fuck her some more. That's how desperate I am to linger inside of her. I crave the feeling of her grip on me when we're together. The aching anticipation of feeling her love me, and then the sound of her crying out my name makes me push harder on the gas petal.

I'm a sick, twisted man. I'm sitting here, driving down this highway with my dick aching in my pants, all because I'm scared to admit to anyone I may not come out of this mission alive. I'm nowhere near ready. She knows it. I know it. And my guys know it. But it's something I have to do. I have to make sure I'm the one who pulls the trigger and looks my own brother in the eyes before I rid the world of his disgusting existence.

"You're a liar." We both look over to each other at the same time. I glance quickly back at the road, then make my turn onto the exit ramp, checking behind me as I come to a complete stop and shove my Jeep into park.

"I fucking told you all I can." Jade glances past me into the dark with her heated stare. A stare that speaks volumes before she even says a word. She knows I'm hiding shit from her; of course she does. How could a brilliant mind like the one she has not? Still doesn't mean she's getting a damn thing out of me.

"I'm not a damn child. Every one of you fuckers are keeping something from me. I knew the minute I saw all of you walking toward me today, with long faces and the same look of deception on every one of you. Is it Ty? Do you know where he is? Has he threatened someone? Hurt someone? Called you? What the hell is it you're trying to protect me from? Because, goddamn it, Kaleb, I'm beginning to think I need protection from you."

What the fuck? Those words bite into my skin, stinging and burning worse than the multiple times my brother actually sliced me open.

She needs protection from me? Protecting her is what I'm trying to do here. Everything I'm doing is to protect her and my family from the malicious monster that is possessed with the evil of Satan, for fuck's sake.

I look away from her. My hands cover the leather steering wheel in a grip that has my hands stinging. I refuse to look at her when she places her hand on my arm. My chest tightens as I replay her words in my head. *Goddamn her.*

The pain shoots up my arm from the death hold I have on the steering wheel, causing the grooves in the leather to dig into my palms. I jerk the vehicle out of park and into drive, and step on the gas a little harder than intended, both of us feeling gravity pulling us back into our seat.

I'm pissed. "Fuck," I spit out, then smash my hand onto the dash. "Goddamn it." She flinches as I yell.

"Stop the fucking Jeep Kaleb. NOW." She yells hysterically in my direction, her anger matching mine. I pull onto the next side road and stop abruptly before she opens the door and slams it. I meet her in front of the Jeep before she has the chance to walk away. She's already headed into the darkness before I can get to her.

"So now you're just going to walk the fuck away into the damn dangers of the night." My voice is loud causing her to spin on her heels to meet me face to face.

"I'm walking away from the danger of riding in that fucking Jeep with you." She spews her angry words in my face before she turns to walk away again. I grab her by the wrist and spin her around not wanting to deal with her attitude while I'm trying to figure out how to handle this fucked up mess.

We both take deep breaths into each other's faces as we stand there with a matching temper. I can feel my heart pounding while my insides start to twist me into an unbearable guttural pain. She's not fucking walking away from me.

"You're not fucking walking away."

"You're not treating me this way." She gets closer to my face and doesn't let up while I take her in. Her eyes are serious and her body screams a fury that I wish I could inhale and take away from her.

"Get the fuck back in my Jeep." My words are deep and demanding. She'll be the death of me with this fucking feistiness.

"Stop acting like a damn idiot and I will."

"I won't ever apologize for trying to protect you, but the last thing you'll ever need is protection from me. I'd never fucking hurt you and you goddamn know it." She lowers down from the height of her tip toes to her normal stance. I watch her as she takes in what I just said.

"You're fucking scaring me. You're keeping shit from me and you think you can just act like an insane lunatic when I say something that doesn't hit you just right. Have you ever thought you might need to listen to what I'm saying?" I don't listen to another word from her, because she can't speak through the connection of my mouth on hers. I pull her against me with a desire to both shut her up and apologize for acting like I have. She pushes against me, so I stop instantly.

We both stare into each other's eyes for a few seconds, our breathing continues to be heavily weighted and I know my mind is all over the place wondering where hers is.

She finally wraps her hands around my neck, pulls me in and aggressively kisses me. It ignites a fire within me that has been stale for far too long. I need her right now. Leaning down just slightly, I lift her so that she's in my arms with her legs around my waist. She continues to kiss me with a hunger and passion that I've missed so much from her. This is my Jade. The woman I first fell for in the desert.

"I'm going to fuck you Jade. I'm not going to think about one fucking thing until I'm done with you." I lean her against the front of my Jeep and sit her on the bull bar before I lift her shirt off of her. This bar makes her perfectly aligned with me and I moan in anticipation of burying myself deep inside of her.

"I've told you once before not to fucking walk away from me. We stand together and fucking face the issue head on." I speak close to her lips and watch her take me in. I've got to her, just like she's got to me. I've never had the intensity I have with her.

She doesn't say another word as she slides her pants off and welcomes my hold on her body as I enter her swiftly. We both adjust with the forcefulness of my thrusts and she grips tight to my body while I hold her close. Two people couldn't be closer than we are right now. This position allows for me to be incredibly deep and it helps that she's practically climbing my body trying to get closer.

I feel her nails scrape across my back while I continue to fuck her in ways I've missed more than I knew. This is the fire I've missed between us. Her passionate kiss causes so many emotions to explode as I transform from a man who's fucking because he's pissed, to a man who can't get enough of the woman in his arms.

"Fuck, Jade. I love how you feel." I stop moving to cherish her in this moment. The night sky is dark all around us, and the sound of cars in the distance. The warmth of the engine making this all even hotter than it usually is between us. I'm sweating my ass off while I continue to fulfill my need of her.

"Please. Don't stop." She moves into my arms and holds herself up with hers around my neck. I grab her hips and slide her easily on and off of me at a fast pace until I'm releasing into her. She follows shortly after. "It's so hot inside." Her words are interrupted as she finishes her orgasm in my arms.

She's so fucking beautiful and I know right now in this moment, I can't let anything happen to her. She's too important for me to risk in any way.

The road leading to her apartment approaches quickly, I'm glad we didn't continue to drive while I was pissed off. These corners would've been a bitch.

"Kaleb." Jade whispers as she meets me in the front of the Jeep once I get out. We didn't actually accomplish anything before we fucked on that dirt road. I know there's still a conversation to be had and I dread every second of it.

She splays her hands wide across my chest while I feel the beating of my heart in my head. I knew she was going to be pissed and act all crazy before. I knew she'd start demanding information wanting to know what the hell is going on, but never in my life did I think she would say something to hurt me. My only focus is keeping her safe, why the fuck would she need protection from me?

"Let's go inside, Jade." She lifts her hands off my chest and moves to the side. I pass her by, stepping into her house. I drop the bags to the floor and hit the light in a robot motion before I run my hands over my face in frustration, trying to decide how to handle this conversation. I'm still so damned pissed I can hardly form a sentence, and somehow I need this stubborn, gorgeous woman to know I love her with everything in me, but I will not sacrifice her safety on a mission like this. My brother is a monster and would love nothing more than to use ammunition like her against me.

I look into her eyes and try like everything to say something that could possibly touch the surface of explaining my love for her. She has me completely choked and I can't speak around the chaos going through my mind. I grab my bag and start walking to the bathroom, hoping a fucking shower will calm me enough to talk to her.

Her voice stops me in my tracks when what she says crashes up against my chest like a roaring wave slamming into you out of nowhere. She's speaking incredibly softly, talking so tenderly through her own restricted voice, and just knowing she's struggling hits my heart instantly.

"I'm sorry. It's just... do you have any idea what ran through my mind when I saw them drag you away from me? I crumbled, Kaleb. I told you how I went ballistic and held a gun to Harris' head. I wasn't in the right state of mind. All I could think about was you and how much I've fallen in love with you. I thought my life was going according to plan when all along my plan was you. I was waiting for you. I used to be as hard on the inside as I am on the outside, and in ways I still am, but not with you. I'm weak when it comes to you, Kaleb. I'm weak because you make me crazy and the thought of ever losing you terrifies me. You make me happy and I don't ever want to lose... "

"Come here," I interrupt her as her words hit home. She couldn't have described our mutual feelings any better. I'm weak when it comes to her, just as she is to me. I'm no expert on love, this is the first and only time I will ever experience it. Jade is it for me. Where I'm about to go could end in a way I'm not prepared to admit, but I have to go into this knowing she is safe, even if it makes her angry.

Reality is a crazy bitch. She'll knock at your doorstep whenever she pleases. Maybe Jade saying what she did was the dose of reality I needed. I need to leave without her knowing. Because the last thing I want to do before I leave is fight with her over this; and that is what we will do if I tell her a damn thing.

I grab her by the waist when she closes in on me and push her up against the wall, allowing my entire body to cover hers again. My hard cock presses into her flat stomach, while we both breathe each other's air again. I lower my face to hers and look straight into her eyes. *Feel me, Jade. Feel everything I can't say and know I'm doing this all for you. For me. I'd lose my fucking mind without you, and there's no way I'm chancing your life for this specific mission. He'll make it personal, and that's something I can't take a gamble on.*

"I'm so sorry." Her words are a strangled whisper, and her soft hands grip my face. I feel her chest heaving up and down as it brushes against mine with every breath. She begins to run her fingers up and down through my beard, tugging on it just before she lets her hands slide down my arms.

"I know you are, but Jade, let me make one thing clear before I take care of you all night long. I want you to know that every single fucking thing I've done since I met you was only done after I thought of how it would affect you. I would never do a goddamn thing to intentionally hurt you. I fucking love you. Do you get me?"

"Yes. I get you. But don't you," she tugs hard on my beard until she has my face within an inch of hers, "ever manhandle me again. You fucking scared me, driving like a lunatic and slamming your fist on the dash. There's a time and a place for taking out your aggression."

"Is that an invitation, Captain?" I bite her bottom lip.

"You bet your sweet ass it is. I happen to like it a little rough if you haven't noticed."

"Now you're challenging me to go again? Jade, baby. I'm sorry too. The last thing I want to do is bring you any more pain. We'll talk about it, just not tonight. Tonight, I need to feel you. To taste you again. To make you forget the hurt and only think about me." Her lips curl up in the naughty way I like. What comes out of her mouth next would have been sufficient enough, but fuck it. I'm a guy. I'll take all I can get, especially from her.

One of her tempting little hands trails down my chest, and she grips a hold of my cock through my jeans, squeezing and teasing. She wants to play again? Hell, I'll always be up for more playtime with her.

"Come on." I grab her hand. My cock is twitching, and jerking, and aching again to come out so quickly. Fuck, I hate fighting with her. Thank god it's done and over.

"Strip." This time, my tone is powerful, demanding as I urge her to take that sexy little outfit off. Jade in her tight camouflage that showcases her tight ass is one thing, but Jade in a tight little shirt and shorts that hug every sinful curve in her body is a tempting sin that she's had me begging to commit all day. She thought the look on my face today when I was stalking toward her after my meeting had to do with the news I heard. She couldn't be more wrong. It had everything to do with her standing on my porch, looking like the sin she is, waiting for me.

I can feel her eyes on me through the darkness, her eager hands rustling around as she slips out of her clothes again. I do the same with my clothes, letting them fall to the floor at my feet.

"Kaleb, take a shower with me." God, I will never get sick of hearing her say my name and hell, yes, I'll shower with her.

"Come here." I don't wait for her. I reach out, grab her wrist, and lead her to her shower. We take our usual quiet shower, all the while using our hands to show our love for one another. She drops to her knees, and before I have time to think, she has me hard and fully erect again. I want us to spend time in bed together, so I shut off the water and lead her to the bed.

Our bodies are soaking wet, but neither of us cares in the slightest. I lie back on her bed and pull her on top of me. My mouth goes to her neck, and I nibble her freshly cleaned skin. I quickly feel her rapid pulse below her ear while she's panting in mine, her noises driving me insane. I'm forgetting, yet memorizing every part of her I can.

"Jesus, Kaleb," she moans.

"Turn around. Take my cock and let me taste your pussy, Jade." The instant she slides herself around, I grip her ass and tug her down onto my face, licking up her center. I fucking growl. Her wet lips start licking the base of my cock, up and down the entire shaft, while I continue to stroke her with my tongue, coaxing her intoxicating smell to impale my senses.

"Fuck." I can't hold back when she swirls her tongue across the tip. She's teasing me, and I can't say I don't love it. I pump my hips up. I want her mouth on me now. I want my come down her throat. I want her all over my cock.

My balls tighten when she slides her wet mouth down my shaft. One of her hands takes over, and she sucks and pumps me hard. She's working me, while I'm working her. I bring her tiny bud in between my teeth and bite down gently, while my fingers move from her ass, spreading her wide, my tongue having the same effect on her as hers does on me. Those noises. Goddamn, those sexy gasps coming out of her have me on the verge of exploding. I lose my shit when she grinds her pussy onto my face. Her taste explodes in my mouth, and there's no way I'm letting that be the way this night ends.

Fucking hell. Welcome to my heaven.

My cock is aching to be inside of her again. I flip her over onto her stomach. "What are you doing?" she asks, her voice raspy and dripping with need.

"I'm going to fuck you, Jade." I use my hand to place her head and shoulders down on the crumpled-up bedding and lift her tight little ass in the air while I listen to her quick breaths and heavy breathing before I slam my cock into her.

"Is this what you wanted? My cock hard, fast, and deep, Jade?" God, she's feels incredible. "Answer me." I fist her hair in my hand and use my other one for support as I rock into her more. Her head snaps up. Her warm breath is right there, begging for me to take her mouth. Not yet. Not until she caves and I rail the shit out of her body. I want to fuck us both into next week.

"I've wanted you since the first time you asked me to get on my knees." *Fuck me.*

"You better come one more time, baby. I'm going to explode inside of you." My hips move my cock in and out of her while she clamps down on me, and I know she's close. God, I'd give anything to see the hunger in her eyes right now.

CHAPTER FIFTEEN

JADE

I wake with a jolt; a deep rush of panic has me feeling alone. "Kaleb." My hands reach behind me to feel his empty, cold side of the bed. Where is he?

We fell asleep with him holding me tightly. It was startling at first, the way he hauled me into his hard body as if he was afraid to let me go. His heart was beating out of control, and I know damn well it had nothing to do with the way he fucked me with such passion and aggression both on the dirt road and in my bed. He's torn up inside, and it's killing me that he won't let me help him.

He woke me a few hours later with nothing but tenderness in his touch. His fingers grazed across my nipple as he whispered in my ear how much he loved me.

Kaleb does love me, but he does not make love. He fucks, and he does it hard. I wouldn't want it any other way with him. I love it when he's rough and takes what is his. He's only made love to me nice and slow a few times, and that was after Afghanistan and before we left for Mexico. I tried not to dwell on it last night. Instead, I felt. I felt his love pouring into me with each passionate thrust, with each desperate kiss. He was trying to get as close to me as he possibly could. The best way he could think of was to be inside of me.

The crazy, dominant, wild Kaleb, who doesn't take no for an answer, took charge when he fucked me twice last night before we went to sleep. Then, as fast as one of my speeding bullets, he flipped and turned on the romance. Romance he swore up and down he doesn't do.

With every deep penetration something followed out of his mouth.

"I'm obsessed with you, Jade." Thrust.

"I could do this with you forever." Thrust.

"I love the way you taste." Thrust.

"Smell." Thrust.

"Feel." Thrust.

It carried on and I loved every minute of it. I became so enamored with his words and his gentle touch the way he stroked me until I felt like I was floating, and then when he kissed my collarbone and buried his head in my neck as he came inside of me, I knew. I fucking knew that whatever he was told in his meeting wasn't good.

And now I'm concerned.

I know I hurt him last night when my anger filtered through my mouth and the words crept out before I had a chance to register what I was saying. If I could take it all back, I would.

I'm dying here though. He's not treating me like his equal or like the soldier I am. He's treating me like he would someone he's trying to protect from the stress of our world. Like a civilian girlfriend, who can't be subjected to the details of a mission like we go on. I'm not fragile. I'm not going to break or shatter. The only way that will happen is if he doesn't quit hiding things and lying to me about whatever the hell is going on.

I need to find him.

Sliding the covers off of me, I swing my legs over the side of the bed. I bend down to grab the first piece of clothing I can find. It's the shirt he had on yesterday. It smells like him. I slip it over my head, turn, and look at the time on the clock. It's four-fifteen. What could possibly have him awake this early? Maybe he's in pain. I know he was yesterday. I saw it every time he switched positions and his back scraped across the couch or chair at his mom's.

I want this nightmare to be over. This is the first real relationship either one of us has been in, and it has been one fight after another to keep us afloat.

"Kaleb," I call out., my hands gliding along the wall for support because of how sore my body is today.

It's eerily quiet. I rush for the light and almost scream when I hear Harris open the front door.

"Fuck, Harris. You scared the shit out of me. Where's Kaleb?" He takes a few steps toward me as I continue to turn more lights on. I really need to get reacquainted with my own apartment. I just haven't stayed here much lately.

"He got called early again. He asked me to keep you with me until he gets back." I know my face turns hard and my words become cold.

I'm fucking angry. After our fight, the rough sex, and then him making love to me, he should've woken me up before he left. He knew there would be a possibility of this and yet, he still kept the mission details from me.

"Are you serious? This pisses me off." I stomp back into the bedroom to get my phone. I can't believe he didn't even have the balls to tell me goodbye. Mexico changed him. It changed us, and I'm not sure I want the kind of relationship where I'm going to always be worried he's going to leave me in the middle of the night on some secret mission.

How am I supposed to have his back when he didn't even make sure I was there to do it? I dial his number, expecting him to send me to voice mail. When he answers, I immediately lose it before 'hello' even comes out of his mouth.

"I can't believe you left without saying goodbye, Kaleb. How do you expect me to be able to breathe until you get back when my mind will be a clusterfuck worrying about you? I saved your ass in Afghanistan. I tried like hell to kill as many as I could in Mexico, while your fucking team pulled away without you." He tries to interrupt me, but I'm so goddamn angry that my words keep spewing out of my mouth. "Then, when you were hanging from a motherfucking tree and the damn Mexicans were pissing on your legs, I'm the one who killed each and every one of them. Your team may be strategic and careful... but I love you. There's not a stronger loyalty than that, Kaleb. How could you just leave me out of this? I know you. I know you're going to find Ty or do something you want me to stay away from. Well, Kaleb. I hate to tell you, I won't tolerate being treated like a fucking fragile little bitch who has to stay at home and keep house while you're out saving the damn world. I don't know what it was about me that made you think I'd sit back and take this without fighting you on it."

"Jade. Stop." His stern words enrage me even more.

"No, Kaleb. You fucking stop. I'm dying here, knowing you're going on a mission and I didn't even get the chance to kiss you goodbye, or to discuss any of this with you. Have you ever thought that this mission may go bad and how I'll feel if I never see you again? You know damn well that could happen on any day in our careers. Just like you wouldn't tolerate me doing this to you, I'm not going to stand by and watch you do this to me."

"What're you saying, Jade?" I stop. What am I saying? Can I deal with this kind of stress on a normal basis? Do I really want to give up everything to be treated like this when I've worked my life to be treated as an equal? If I can't even get that in my relationship, how do I expect to get it in my career?

"I can't do this, Kaleb. I love you, but I can't live like this." His silence is gutting me. My tears slide down my face with anger and sadness as I tell him what I wish like hell I didn't have to. But I have to remember who I am in this. I have no idea where to find him or how to help him, and I'll be absolutely consumed with worry until I hear they made it back, but I'll have to distance myself from him in the future. He's forcing that on me with his actions.

I hate to do this over the phone, and I really despise fighting with him before he leaves on a mission. I may not be able to have a real relationship with him, but that doesn't change the fact I fucking love this man and I'll be totally destroyed from all of this. "Please, just be safe. I'll be here when you get back." I lie. I can't have him out there doing his job and worrying about us at the same time. For his safety and for my heart right now in this moment, he needs to think we'll be alright.

"Jade. I wish like fuck I could tell you." Every time he talks, another piece of my heart breaks.

"We both know you could, you just choose not to. But I understand." I'm trying like hell to be sympathetic here. I swallow hard, holding my chest with my free hand, while I fight through the giant lump in my throat to end this call. "I love you, Kaleb. I'll see you soon." I close my eyes and stop breathing as I wait for his response. His voice is raspy and uncertain when he finally speaks.

"I love you too, baby. Just tell me we'll work through this when I get back. Because I am coming back, Jade. I'm coming back to you." The tears escape fast as I squeeze my eyes closed tightly, knowing I can't ever see him again.

"I'll be here. Please be safe." I hit end and sit on the edge of the bed, feeling the weight of the words from the call. My heart hurts, and I know I'm right about not being able to see him again. He has always had a way of owning me when he's near me. If I let him get close to me, I know exactly what he'll try to do. He'll coax me with his ability to strip me bare, because that's exactly what he's done. He's left me exposed, naked in a way I may never recover from. Kaleb Maverick has peeled away the hard shell I've had guarding my heart, and now he's left me bleeding.

I hear Harris' footsteps as he walks to the doorway, stopping to lean against it after he asks me, "You alright?"

"No, I'm not. He's treating me like a civilian girlfriend he can't share shit with. Or hell, it could be worse. Is he just doing this to keep me from going because he's trying to protect me? Either way, I can't do this for the rest of my life. I've worked my ass off to prove I'm capable of being strong and that I'm not afraid to take out any enemy or threat in the way of completing a mission. So what if I got pissed at the team for taking off without him? I would've been pissed to leave anyone there. I mean, hell, we just left him there to be eaten alive by the enemy." I stand and start to pace back and forth as I talk. "He's hiding something from me, and I can't deal with that. What did he say to you exactly?"

"He asked me to keep you safe until he returned. I told him I would. That's it. Jade. You know we don't ask questions. We just do as we're told. You should be used to this by now."

"This isn't the Army. He's not our commanding officer anymore. He's our fucking teammate. This is my relationship with the man I love. How am I supposed to stay here, knowing he's going into some deep shit? I'm losing my mind, thinking about all the possibilities of what can go wrong. What if those guys don't watch every single fucking thing, Harris? I can't do this every day. This is not a life I want to lead. I'm built to fight, not keep fucking house."

"Are you seriously walking away from him?" I stop moving and stand silent as I look at Harris still leaning against the doorframe.

"I have to, Harris." I sit on the edge of the bed again before I realize I'm sitting here only in Kaleb's t-shirt.

"Damn it. I'm losing my mind. I'm prancing around here in a damn t-shirt in front of you."

"I've seen it all before. I know it's not like that." He shrugs like it's no big deal, but it is to me. This is part of what I mean about being naked and bare. He has my mind fucked up with worry, and I feel vulnerable to the fact that my whole life could be changed with one wrong move by any of them.

I slide some shorts and have to roll the waist down so they'll stay up on my hips. Harris never leaves his spot, and I want to yell at him at the same time I want to thank him for always being here.

"No, it's not." I grab a brush, running it through my tangled-up hair, gathering it up, and securing it with a few pins into a messy bun while I start to think about what I'm going to do from here.

"Tell me where your head is, Elliott. I need to know the plan before you move on anything." I busy myself picking up everything on the floor, which isn't much.

"We're leaving here. I'll report in tomorrow and see if they can get me back out there."

"You really think rushing back out there is going to help you through all of this?"

"It can't hurt." He pushes off the wall and moves toward me.

"You're not ready for that, and you know it."

"Well, Harris. I'm not going to just sit around and play housewife. That's not who I am. He obviously wants that from me." I leave the bedroom to get the last of my stuff gathered. I want Harris to get me out of here before I break down and cry again.

Throwing the last of my stuff in my bag, I flip the lights off and start past him to the door. He steps in front of me, stopping me in my tracks.

"Stop. I'm not going to let you make any rash decisions until we know exactly what's going on. I'm taking you to the ranch for a few days, so you can chill the fuck out. I've already told our superior where we'll be. He agreed on the extended R&R for both of us. You have to call him yourself and let him know your whereabouts." I look at his chest, because honestly, my eyes can't look into his. His caring demeanor is something that's easy for me to pull toward when I'm hurting like this. He's been through so much with me, and I continue to send him on a ride from hell with the chaos in my life. I know him well enough to know he wouldn't have it any other way, but hell, I need to feel some sense of normalcy soon before I lose my mind.

"I have Mallory packing her bag at my house. She's coming with us." I look up. His eyes are soft, and he grins just slightly when I start quizzing him.

"You fucking my friend, Harris? Because I swear I can't deal with her heart being broken when I'm dealing with my own shattered mess."

"We're just having fun. Now, give me your bag. Call your superior and tell him where you're going." He reaches for my single bag just like the gentleman he is.

"Fun, huh. So I'm about to be a third wheel on a fuck fest weekend with the two of you."

"No, I'll keep it to a minimum just for you. Now, get your ass in my truck. You need a few days to truly relax, and I'm going to make that happen for you if I have to strap you to a lounge chair myself." I follow his large stature as I hit the last light in the house. Closing my eyes as I do doesn't help the hurt. Breathing slowly as I walk the path Harris is leading, I whisper, "Goodbye, Kaleb," as I close the door to my apartment and any possibility of a future with him.

CHAPTER SIXTEEN

KALEB

Fuck. I throw my phone on the floor in front of the passenger seat in frustration. She's leaving me. I could hear it in her fucking voice. This is something I can't compromise on, so I'm left with only one choice. Deal with the fate of us once I get back. I'd rather know I have a for sure chance to have that conversation by keeping her safe over taking her with me and chancing my brother torturing me by ruining her. I could never live with myself if that happened.

Her words echo through my head as I reach the airport and they don't stop replaying the entire flight to the compound. It's the longest flight of my life.

I know her well enough to know the end of that conversation was her way of making me feel like there's going to be something to come back to. Well, I hate to tell her stubborn ass I'm not letting this end us. She can try to walk away from me all she wants, but I will find her with the tracker in her damn leg, and when I do, I know how she'll react to me. Just like how I'm pulled to her, she's drawn to me, no matter how hard she tries to fight it. She may as well not even try it. It didn't work in the desert and it won't work now.

I land, and I'm still pissed off in more ways than one. She hasn't messaged me, but I didn't expect her to. I'm desperately fighting the urge to fly right back to her and just tell her everything, but I won't.

"That was a quick trip. Great plan to get Jade out of here, my friend. How'd she take you leaving her behind?" Jackson must've drawn the short stick, because he's the one here to pick me up.

"Not good." His fucking laughter fills the cab, so I give him a death glare to show him I'm not in the mood to deal with any laughter or jokes today.

"I bet she didn't." He pulls the truck out of the pick-up lane before he starts in on me again.

"You know. She's changed you." I cross my arms, knowing he's right, but not wanting to hear anything right now except the sound of my brother's last breath.

"Jackson. Not today. Today, I need you to work and not talk. I need to get this done so I can get my ass back to her asap."

"10-4 ,big guy. I read you loud and clear." I hate to be a dick to him. He's one hell of a guy. He's just one to joke all the time, and right now, I'm not feeling like being poked at.

The rest of the ride is quiet, and I begin to get in the mindset that I'll need to be in whenever I come face-to-face with my brother. I hope like hell he's here in the States. I'd love nothing more than to meet him in my territory, where I can make the rules.

The early morning phone call from Kase has my head exploding. One minute, we're waiting for clearance to head back to Mexico; then the next, we're not. Fucking scared the piss out of me when I saw his name flashing on my screen. Good thing I was awake and she was passed out from exhaustion. I hopped out of her bed as quickly as I could before answering, and then shut myself in the bathroom like some school kid hiding out.

I'll hold on to the memories of having everything to do with her being so exhausted. I just wish I could've woken up with her in my arms. Then it all hits me. There's a possibility I'll never see her again. She may never let me touch her again. I swallow hard with the realization and try to focus on the positive.

I should be relieved we aren't heading to Mexico and that I don't have to leave Jade behind while I go back there and relive my nightmare all over again on top of worrying about her back here.

But fuck, when Kase said the Mexican authorities would handle it and under no circumstances did they want the United States government involved, that shit worries me even more. Then he drops the bomb that my brother has been spotted near the US border and I need to get back to headquarters immediately.

There is no way in hell Ty would be there when they go in, whenever that will be. Assholes like him have people on the inside. I bet anything he has several of them on his payroll. The fucker is long gone by now.

That's why I immediately called Harris the second I hung up with Kase. He's the only one I trust to keep her safe. I told him to talk her into going to the ranch. It's the safest place for her right now. This whole thing is out of my control, and it's making me fucking crazy. Control is my middle name. I have to have it, and when I don't, I get shitty.

I reach for my phone on the floor as we pull into the gates of the compound. Fucking Jackson and his crazy-ass driving. Swerving all over the place like an asshole.

I glance at the screen one more time, just in case I missed a call or message from her when I was off in my own little world, only to find nothing. *Fuck.*

My phone starts to vibrate in my hand, and I quickly see that it's my mom.

"Hi, mom. What's up?"

"Your brother called, Kaleb." Her words are barely audible through the sobs I can hear and the pain flowing from her. My heart instantly freezes.

"How did he get through? Your number was changed years ago, mom." God. I need her here with me. The sounds of her sobbing achingly are killing me. I can't imagine what's running through her mind right now.

"He called the neighbor. He took a message and just brought it over. What do you want me to do?"

"Mom. I need you to calm down, please. I know this is a shock to you after all this time. Please trust me when I tell you Ty is a dangerous man. I need you focused right now. Tell me what he said, mom?" I'm about to lose my shit as I think about that motherfucker getting anywhere near my family. I should've forced her to move to the compound. *Fuck.*

My hands start shaking as I glance over to Jackson, whose expression is pinched. Worry is creasing his features and his fists are clenched while he begins to shake too.

"He said he'll be coming to visit soon and wanted to make sure I had his number. My neighbor, Rick, wrote it out. I have it if you want me to call him."

"Fuck, no, mom. Don't you dare call and talk to his ass. I'll have you and Amelie moved immediately. Ty is into some deep shit, and I can't chance he'll bring it to your fucking door."

"Kaleb Maverick. Quick saying 'fuck' to your mother. Is this what you were not telling me the other day? Do you have more information on Ty I need to know about?" *Yeah, mom. I have a lot of information about your son.* I'm not about to tell her that though.

"We'll talk as soon as you get here. Grab a bag and get a few things. I'll have a flight arranged in about five minutes. My security guys will get you from the house. Mom. I need you to move fast. Leave everything as it is and get the hell out of there."

"Alright. I'm moving." Now her voice turns panicky. "Where's Amelie?" I close my eyes, hoping to god she's called her already.

"She's here." Thank you, god.

"One more thing. The only word they are going to say to you is 'Fire' when they come to the door. They won't say anything else. If they don't, then you tell Amelie to take that shotgun and blow their heads off, do you understand me? I have to go. I'll see you soon. Text me the number he left you." I hang up on her, knowing I need to get them out of there now. My heart is panicked, and I'm pissed I let her convince me he'd leave her alone. This could just be a threat to me, because he knows she'll call me with the information if he contacts her. This is him playing games. Well, game on, motherfucker.

I work fast to get everyone in place and a plan set out for them to get to me, while Jackson heads inside.

My next call is to Harris to check on Jade.

"Tell me you're already on the move." I don't even give him the chance to greet me.

"Sure am. Already on the road. Figured a road trip might do us some good again. What's up?" He sounds at ease, and I find peace in knowing he's got her.

"Nothing. Just stick with the plan and keep me posted." I trust Harris, but he needs to know this is a hell of a lot more serious than it was when I called him earlier.

"How's she doing?" I'm surprised my voice is as calm as it is with all the shit that's running through my head right now.

"Been better." I can tell he's trying to keep his words short, but to the point. She's right there with him.

"I'm going to make this right. Just please, stay with her. My brother called my mom today. He's circling the area, and I need her safe and nowhere near me." Ty will never be able to put her with me when she's across the country. That ranch is well hidden and a perfect place for her to go.

"We're good here. Do what you have to do."

"Thanks, Harris." I leave those as my parting words and climb up the steps into the office. The feeling of panic completely outweighs how thankful I am, but I'm determined. Panic and determination; that's a lethal combination right there.

"Alright. Let's gather around the table. We don't have any spare time until we find my brother. The President wasn't interested in starting a war with the Mexican Cartel, so we're on our own with this." I'm livid, and no one says a damn word as they all gather around.

"You sure you want to start this, Fire? Once we do this, there's no turning back." Kase is just making sure I'm thinking with a level head, and I'm sure he's worried about the fallback from this if we find Ty's whereabouts. This shit is deep. He's now coming into my territory, and I need a fucking game plan for when he arrives. I know damn well he will. This could fall on all of our shoulders if we don't find him, because he will start picking apart everyone we love to get to Al-Quaren. I know he needs him. I'd love nothing more than to give the fucker back to him and not be worried about the safety of every single person I care about, but that isn't how all of this works.

"You know damn well he'll be coming for us to get Al-Quaren back. He has to. I know without a doubt that was Fernando pressuring him on the phone when he held me captive. They were talking about missed firearm shipments over him losing that terrorist fucker to us. He has orders to get him back, or his fucking life is ruined." My temper flares at how he's fucked up his life.

"Who's to say he's not already in the States?" Vice speaks up and I welcome his thoughts. Hell, I've thought them a million times myself in the past few days.

I practically stop breathing when I think he contacted my family, but now that I know they're on a plane coming straight for me, maybe I'll be able to calm down soon. I'll have to get them settled here, so I can go find my brother. We'll have the best team looking for any sign of his whereabouts. Fucker will have to show his face one time or another.

I wish I didn't have to leave once they get here, but I can't be everywhere, even though I wish I could be. No. I need to be the one to put an end to my brother. I have to trust that everyone else keeps up their side of this mess and protects those I love.

"Nothing says that. He could be anywhere, but I'd put my life on the fact he's here. Especially since he contacted your mom." Pierce stands up then works to fix the projector so that our satellite imaging is displayed. I turn to Jackson and nod my thanks for him letting them know about the call from my brother. Saves us time we do not have if I had to explain what the hell happened. I let Pierce take the floor and begin the details of our plan.

"I have my intel team working on anything they can find on him." Kase leans forward in his chair, pulling out his phone to continue texting, while data scans across his computer screen.

"Alright. We need anything and everything we know about him brought to the damn table now. His name is Tyler Daniel Maverick. Aka Robert Daniels. Aka Danny B. Have them run all of those names and pull up the American from the sex slave case we worked. See if any of the details match." I start barking orders and everyone moves quickly. This is why I love my team. These table meetings bring out the best of all of us.

"Also, get me the feed to all of the GPS trackers. I want to know where everyone is during all of this." Pierce hits a few buttons, and a map of the United States pops up with tiny red dots flashing in three areas.

"Looks like Jade must be traveling. We've got our other guys in North Carolina waiting for word to move." Pierce points to the screen, but my eyes zone in on her flashing dot. That's right, baby, get your ass to that ranch.

"I discovered a little something, or should I say, our handy friends down there did." Pierce turns his head in my direction with remorse and sympathy etched across his face.

"Spill it." My brows furrow, then I look at the screen, immediately understanding why he's looking at me the way he is.

"Is that what I think it is?" Kase stands, his big build hovering in front of the screen.

"My god. That's where they were holding me. Fuck me." Every damn second of the torture and my brother's face flash before my eyes when Kase moves out of the way. The shithole structure of a building and that wicked tree are on the screen. Only this time, I can see. Clear as can be. My eyes aren't half open, and there's no darkness from the recordings that night. There's a large structure just behind all of that, half hidden in the trees. He zooms in behind it, and I work to make out what I'm seeing.

"It's fucking cages. The asshole has cages. Are those people?" Shit, I can't fucking see it zoomed in that far.

"Give me a second." I listen to Pierce tap on the keyboard and freeze when the image comes back up. I hear my team moan, and I want to kill that motherfucker.

"Scan the whole area." I need to see everything. He moves across the metal building, and I can see a few trucks in the back, probably loading something up. "What's the time stamp on this satellite image, Pierce?"

"Three days ago." Fuck. He continues to scan the area, only to show us the tops of the buildings and the surrounding fields.

"That has to be his hiding place for god knows what, and it's surrounded by a motherfucking poppy plantation. The flowers are everywhere." I can't stand how close I was to this shit. Who knows who he has caged up, but I'll be damned if I'll let them be there much longer. "Get this information to the Mexican police contact we have. Fuck. I can't believe he's involved in all of this."

"We walked right past that shit," Jackson speaks up.

"Yeah, well, at the time, this wasn't our priority," Kase says, pointing at the screen.

"No. It wasn't. I can say this though. If I had known that shit was there, I would've taken care of those cages before I torched that motherfucking structure to the ground. Jesus Christ, man, you good with this, brother? You sure you can handle this?" Kase tilts his head down and looks me directly in the eyes.

I don't need to sit here and contemplate my answer. I've had weeks to think about when and how I would destroy Ty. Years, really, when it comes down to it. He just topped off my feelings for him when he chose to brutalize me, leaving parts of my body scarred for life. He's hurt our mom in a way she'll never recover from, then calling her like he's coming for a fucking visit when he's a damn monster now. Goddamn right, I'm ready.

"I'm good. Let's figure this shit out. I told Jade I'd take her away on a vacation one day, and that's a promise I tend to keep." I don't lead them to believe anything other than that Jade and I are perfect right now. They don't need to know the deepest parts of my gut worry about her once I get back to her.

I stand up along with my brothers, while Kase pulls up all the information he was given on Fernando. I just hope to god I can come face-to-face with Ty and watch his expression as we crumble his fucking world.

I can hardly stay focused. All I see is drugs, guns, illegal immigrants, sex slavery. Every damn thing our country fights to stay free of. Newspaper clippings, possible sightings of this notorious man who seems to be moving from one location to another.

They've been after my brother for several years. And it's no wonder I had no clue or never once saw his face in any news article or television report. In every photo, his head is down or turned away. But it's him. I'd know his voice and his posture anywhere. He's been hiding his identity when he has to step out.

How in the hell could he go from a drug user to one of the biggest smugglers of everything illegal like this? I'm floored. This cuts deep. So fucking deep I can hardly breathe, knowing I share the same blood as this man.

I place my head in my hands. Ever since I found out it was him, I've been trying to convince myself I wanted to destroy him, hurt him in the same way he's hurt us. I need to wipe his body from the earth and pretend like he never existed.

I'm a hardass and a man of my word, but somehow, I'm a brother to a man who has committed horrendous crimes I can't even fathom. He's my goddamn brother, and no matter how hard I try to convince myself the torture he's put me through and the half-empty life he's left my mother to lead gives him reason to die, it still doesn't settle well with me. The rage I've felt for him for everything he's done still boils in me, but the fact remains... he's my mother's son. He's my brother. I need a damn moment to grieve the fact the boy I knew is already truly dead. This man walking around in his body isn't the kid I grew up with.

I've tried to tell myself he was already dead to us, but seeing his face on this monitor, hearing his voice call out commands, and watch his men deliver his demands creates a whole new array of feelings. I wish I could break through the lies that have become his fucked-up life, to make him see, just one damn time, that I tried, god only knows I tried. And I failed him.

"Kaleb." I snap my head up, my eyes blazing at Pierce.

"This shit isn't on you, brother. It's on him. Don't rile yourself up. You tried to help him. He chose this, not you." I know he's trying to help me see things for what they really are. I figured that out years ago. It's seeing all this new information that has me wishing he would've listened to me. I could've saved him, and now I have to kill him.

"I'm good. Let's finish this up. Figure out where they could be hiding and find out if he's here in the States or not. This needs to be put to rest."

"The last known place this Fernando was spotted was in Columbia. That was two weeks ago. It's like he's fallen off the radar after that until last night," Kase points out.

"Of course, he did. This is a domino effect, man. He'll hide out again for a while. He may even disappear and let Fernando take the fall. You know damn well he knows he's been narked on. Shit, this is the closest he's come to being caught." Steele, always the smart one, tells us like it is.

"Yeah, well. That shit is on the government, man. My concern is finding Ty. None of that shit gives you a clue at all? I mean, hell, they have to know something," I stand again and point directly to the same monitor, the same sheets of paper, maps, and endless notes we've all been looking at for hours.

"Our hands are tied until Mexico gets back with our authorities. We can't do shit about Fernando, but we have a phone number for your fucking brother. I say call his ass." Jackson leans back in his chair, grinning like he's looking forward to the call.

I've already thought about calling him if we were somehow able to track down a number for him. I just wanted to make sure I had everyone safe before I got him on the phone. I know it's not going to end on a good note, so I'm playing it safe.

"I will the second my mom and sister land. Until then, I don't want him to know I'm onto his ass.

CHAPTER SEVENTEEN

JADE

The road is never ending, and even though I've done nothing but sleep, the time doesn't seem to be passing fast enough. I feel confined, and my mind won't stop thinking about Kaleb. He's the most stubborn man, and I wish like hell I hadn't fallen so hard for him. I really thought I had gained his respect and wouldn't ever have to face him treating me any different because we grew closer. It's like just because of our connection, he's shutting me out on this mission. I'm sure it's hit him that it all changes when someone you love is in danger.

It's just different. I learned that very quickly in Mexico. I mean, I've always loved my brothers, both in and out of the Army, but what I have with Kaleb goes much deeper. Where I'd be devastated if I lost a brother in action, I'd be completely ruined if anything happened to Kaleb. He's my weakness. I wanted him to remain my strength because when we first got together, he was. He built me up, only to throw me down when he felt I didn't need to be involved anymore.

I wipe a tear from my cheek when Harris' phone rings. I listen to him vague talk his way through a conversation I'm sure Kaleb is on the other end of. Tucking my hoodie back into the corner of the window, I close my eyes and try to ignore everything.

"That was Kaleb. He asked about you." Harris' voice forces my eyes open.

"What did you tell him?"

"I told him you've been better." He looks over at Mallory in the front seat, then back at me.

"I'll be fine. Don't tell him shit about me, Harris. If he wants to know how I am, he can call me." I lay my head back into the sweatshirt before he responds.

"Would you fucking answer his call, Jade?"

"Yes." I would answer his call, but I won't see him. I don't add that part because I know Harris is all team Kaleb now.

"You know you're being stubborn, and if he doesn't kick your ass, I will. He's doing what he has to do."

"Harris. Since when did you know me as the stay-at-home type? Would you really push me to stay with someone who isn't going to treat me with the respect I deserve?"

"Elliott. You have no idea how much that man respects you. Just don't count him out till this mission is over. He'll be back and you two can talk about your issues. You had to know it would be a difficult relationship when you got together."

"Seriously, Jade. Don't let a man treat you any other way than you deserve." Mallory sits up and turns to look at me.

"Mal. He's protecting her. I promise you would approve."

"What exactly are you being protected from, Jade? Should I be worried about you? All of these trips to the middle of nowhere... I'm just concerned." And I know just how she feels now. Being on the outside of the information sucks, and just like I know I can't tell her, she knows that too.

"This sucks." She flops back in her seat and rolls down her window, letting the cool air hit us both.

"I know it does, but it's just the way it is." Harris adds his insight that neither of us wants to hear for our own reasons. We all remain quiet for the remainder of the drive, only making one more stop along the way.

He pulls up to the ranch, and we all quietly make our way through the front door.

"I'm going to bed. I'll see you both in the morning." Even though I've been sleeping most of the day, I'm just not in the mood for small talk or pretending to be anything I don't want to be.

With my clothes still on, I slide into the same bed Kaleb and I shared the last time we were here. His pillow smells only faintly like his cologne, and I consider how twisted I am that I'm pulling it close to me to cuddle. I'm literally torturing myself here, but this doesn't even come close to cuddling with him. To feel his warm body holding me, knowing he's safe, would be the perfect scenario. I felt safe and comforted with him, and now all I feel is worry. This is something I'll have to get used to.

I hear my phone vibrate on the bedside table, where seconds ago I placed it, and reach for it quickly. It's a text from him.

Kaleb: I love you, Jade.

I contemplate my response while my tears swell in my eyes. Damn it. I've cried more in the past few weeks than I have in my life. My mind starts flashing through the first time I met Kaleb Maverick all the way to today. His powerful being consumed me from his first touch and never released me. I'm just so confused about all of this, and I'm not sure what I want to do with the rest of my life when it comes to him. One minute, I want to give him up; the next, I want to track his ass down. I hate feeling like I'm tangled up in a hundred different ropes, trying to loop one over the other to try to get free.

Hell, I have no idea if he's even in Mexico, Missouri, Florida, or deep in a desert in Afghanistan.

I want to reply, because I do love him. I want to be the woman he needs me to be, but I can't. Leaving me out of major plans is not an option. I'd rather be single than fear every moment of the unknown that would come with being with Kaleb. I type the four words, then erase them three times before I set my phone back on the table. He's safe. Or he wouldn't be texting. That's all I need to know.

I hug his pillow tighter and let the tears fall freely as I try to make sense of what I'm going to do tomorrow. "I love you too, Kaleb."

I cry myself to sleep and say a silent prayer that all of the guys are safe tonight.

******

I wake to a hand covering my face and try to scream past the rag. A hand is firmly pressed against my mouth, and another one grips my throat. I panic because I'm struggling to breathe. My quick response only makes it worse, because now, this fucker is in bed with me. I feel a hard erection press into my back and fight to free myself from his hold, but my body won't move fast enough.

Shit, my eyes go wide. I'm gliding, falling. *I've been drugged.*

KALEB

I had to text her. I know she was still up because Harris had just sent the text saying they had arrived at the ranch. His reply that she's already in bed only tells me she's depressed as fuck, and that frustrates me. I'm not pissed at her, I'm mad at this whole situation. Jade and I have never had an easy day in our relationship. We've had a lot to deal with, but I know it'll all work out. It has to. She's the perfect person for me.

I watch my phone for ten minutes, hoping she'll reply, but she doesn't. She saw it. I know she did. I know I pissed her off with this mission, but I originally thought we were going to Mexico. Now, we're stuck at the compound, playing a waiting game, and I could've had her in my arms tonight, but instead she's alone. *Fuck, Jade. Reply to me.*

My mom and sister took the guest bedrooms in the house. It tore out that last bit of my guts to see them step off of the plane, both of them with red, puffy eyes, hurt and confusion coating their entire demeanor. My mom lost it again and began pounding me with questions I had no clue how to answer. Her two sons are fighting against each other, and both have the desire to kill the other. How the hell do you look at the woman who brought you into this world and tell her what one of her children's lives has become? I told her the minimal. Of course, she blew up, demanding me to tell her more. I couldn't. I may never be able to. If it wasn't for my sister stepping in to help me calm her down, I would still be up, trying to figure out what to say to her, while listening to her heart being ripped out of her chest all over again.

Even though they're all safe tonight, I can't sleep, so I'm out on the porch, drowning in the sound of the night. My phone is in my lap, and I'm trying like hell to not fucking wake Steele up and make him fly my ass to Alabama to see her. *Goddammit, Jade.*

I stretch my arms behind me and watch the sunrise from the middle of the porch. The sky is beautiful even though half the sky is being shadowed with a large storm cloud. The other side is sunlit and causing a contrasting flare to the darkness.

"You up already?" Jackson stops running as he approaches.

"No. Haven't slept yet."

"Fuck, man. You know that's not good. You need to rest, Kaleb."

"I know. Too much on my mind."

"Jade or your brother?"

"Both. Hell, you take a pick."

"Have you heard from her?"

"Yeah, Harris said they made it. She went straight to bed."

"Damn, man. You know why she's pissed, right? You have to know her well enough to know how to fix this."

"I will. Just need to handle some family business before I bring her into it."

"You guys need that vacation when this is all over."

"I agree. I'm taking her away for a few weeks when I get the chance."

"My man. You're gonna just have to create the chance. I've known you for years, and you're always working." I exhale. I know he's right. I'd love more than anything to slow down some and make a life with Jade. I just don't know if I have it in me to slow down.

He sits next to me and leans the chair back on two legs. "Your ass will come back with triplets if you take her away for a week." I smile at the thought of Jade pregnant with my baby, knowing our lives would forever be changed with news like that. There's no way in hell we're anywhere ready for that to happen.

"Ah. We won't be having any little Fires for a long while."

"Thank god, man. The big Fire is enough." His laughter comforts me. Jackson is always a happy guy. He's learning timing is crucial for me. "You ready to call that asshole brother of yours, now that your mom is safe?" I catch some anxiousness as well as the seriousness this man rarely shows.

"Yes, I am. Not that he'll tell me where he is." He's a chicken shit. I don't have to express that for Jackson to know this. It's obvious.

"You'd be surprised. He may give us a clue. We can always try to track him, but I'm sure he's smarter than that shit."

"He is." How the hell he became smart when his entire life he's been nothing but a dumb fuck is a riddle to me.

"Let's get the guys around the table and call his ass now."

"Alright, gather them up. I'll be right there." He stands quickly and starts jogging toward the main office, where we keep all the computer equipment. We'll record this call and analyze the fuck out of it. I wouldn't be surprised if Pierce finds him based on this call. He's a sharp motherfucker and someone I wouldn't want to hide from. He's an expert at that shit.

"Dial that fucker. Everyone stay completely quiet until the call is ended." Pierce sets all the equipment to record, and I dial my sick fucking brother. The phone rings four times, and I start to worry he won't answer. Then he picks up the call.

"I knew you'd call. Surprised it took you this long." His voice disgusts me, and I battle the urge to scream at him for the shit he's in on.

"What do you want? You know I'll kill you before you get a chance to go near mom or Amelie." His laughter is evil. Like the protégé of the devil himself. I send looks around the room as we try to analyze his reactions to me. He thinks he scares me. He's far from it.

"Believe me. I won't be needing mom or Amelie. That phone call was a distraction." I can hear a grin on his face as he speaks even louder into the phone. What the hell does he mean by that? I go to speak, but he quickly cuts me off. His next words leave me with a gaping hole in my chest.

"You see, brother. You made one mistake. You fell in love." I stand instantly, wondering what the fuck he's talking about, refusing to believe his distraction has anything to do with Jade. Pierce moves quietly through the screens to pull up the trackers, and my fucking heart stops beating. She's not at the ranch. *Fuck.*

I try to compose my anger and work this call like a professional as I watch the reactions of every single one of the guys. They all know what this means. *He has her.*

"I don't know what you're talking about." I'm shaking. My muscles are contracting. I close my eyes and play dumb every time I open my mouth even though my mind has already put together the situation.

"Play games with someone else, Kaleb. Bring me Al-Quaren or say goodbye to your precious blonde here with the nice tits." Jesus. What has he done?

"You fucking dick. I'll cut your goddamn head off and piss down your throat If you so much as touch her." I'm losing my shit here. He has my weakness. The fucker is spearing me in the heart, and he knows it.

"Oh, big brother. I'm not interested in your threats. Bring me Al-Quaren, or the next time you hear me talk.... It'll be while I'm fucking her with my dick buried deep inside this sweet pussy of yours. In fact, I'm staring at her long legs and these toned arms... Ohhhh, fuck, and this beautiful face I can just imagine what it'll look like when I'm deep inside her. I must say I'm impressed. I bet she tastes as sweet as she looks. I can almost see it now. Me on top of her, while she fights to get away from me. Then I can fuck and choke the life out of her." My skin erupts. My heart explodes, and my head bursts with the thought of Ty having Jade. *What the fuck have I done?* I can't think straight.

"I'm warning you, Ty. Stay the hell away from her. And you know I can't bring you a terrorist that's in US custody."

"You'd better figure something out. I'll give you six hours to send me a video that proves you have him before I kill her. Until then... I believe I'll play with this ball of fire. Tell me, Kaleb.... Does she enjoy it in the ass?" My insides twist, and I swear to god my heart is no longer beating as I think of him touching her anywhere.

"Ty, I swear on my life, if you so much as breathe on her, I'll torture you in ways you've never imagined." He ends the call like the coward he is, and I grip the edge of the table and roar the loudest, animalistic sound I've ever heard. All of the guys are moving around, either hitting keyboards or packing bags. I'm fucking furious. I've never felt disgust and repulsion like I feel right now. This filth is related to me. And to think, when I found out earlier about all the shit he's involved in, it actually tore me to shreds to think I failed him. He brought this war on himself. He destroyed his family and his own life, not me. I fucking hate him.

"He fucking has Jade. What in the goddamn fuck? Tell me how to fucking breathe."

Peirce's logical voice is louder than mine. "Move your ass, Kaleb. We have Steele already fired up, and I've got Vice and Ace already positioned with your mom and sister. He doesn't know we have the tracker in Jade's leg. We go to him. He doesn't have a chance in hell. Get your fucking shit together or I'm pulling you from this." I challenge him with my glare. He knows better than to try to keep me from going.

"Don't look at me like you're the one in charge here. He may have the woman you love, but man, if you don't put that aside and treat this like any other mission, I will leave you here. Now, pull your damn shit together. We find where he has her. We kill him and we move the fuck on." I let his words sink in, knowing he's right. The only thing he's forgetting is once I know we have Jade; I'm going to kill him slowly. I'm going to bring pleasure to myself by torturing the hell out of him and make him wish he were never fucking born.

CHAPTER EIGHTEEN

JADE

The burn of the rope pulling tight on my wrists wakes me. The struggle to break free only rips my tender flesh even more. I cringe from the sting soaring up my arm and into my shoulders and stiff neck. The room is mostly dark, the only light coming from a small window, and I'm searching for any sign of who might have me.

I hold my breath with the movement of someone behind me, only exhaling slowly when I hear him talk. "Morning, sunshine. Do you always talk in your sleep?" His voice is deep and familiar, with a gritty edge to it. He's directly behind me, his warm breath at the base of my ear.

God, this has to be Ty. There isn't anyone else who would dare to come face-to-face with two military experts. My eyes go frantic, and I try to tilt my head to look at the bastard. I'm not concerned about me right now. I need to know how the hell he got past Harris and Mallory. Did he shoot them? Hurt them? Are they still alive?

God, no. Kaleb would never forgive himself if something happened to either one of them.

And me. I left them. More concerned for myself than staying up and visiting with them. I'm to blame if anything has happened to them. I need to stay calm and analyze this damn situation I have myself in. He wants me weak. He wants me frantic and begging, I can appear weak and play his game.

I listen to his heavy breathing continue in my ear as he slides his hands down my chest. His slimy fingers travel lower, and I squirm with hatred as he palms both of my breasts, pinching and squeezing my nipples. He's getting off on this, while I'm ready to vomit. My chest heaves up and down, while his breathing becomes heavier and more erratic.

I'm battling to stay quiet when all I want to do is scream at him through the tape he has across my mouth. He needs to get his filthy hands off of me. I'd love to tell him he's fucked up in a way that's going to cost him his life, but I don't say a word. I remain quiet, desperately trying to forget the fact his touch is repulsing me.

He's tied my feet to the legs of the chair and my wrists together behind my back. He's leaving me completely vulnerable to his twisted fucking ways, and I want nothing more than to kill him in ways that would make Kaleb's torture seem like a walk in the park.

"I'll have to thank my brother for taking you to meet the family. I knew he'd go to mom's. I just didn't expect him to bring so much baggage." He removes his hands before he slithers in front of me with a smug look on his face.

I wish like crazy I had seen him in Mexico. I would've put a bullet right in his dick too, before I blew his head off. He's the poster boy for white fucking trash.

He looks like Kaleb in a way, but like he's five years older. He's the younger brother, so I know his lifestyle has been rough on his appearance. Having drug lords up your ass will do that to you.

They have similar yet different eyes. Where Kaleb's are warm and full of love when he looks at me, Ty's are dark, and hatred trails all the way to the wrinkles swarming his deadly eyes. They're just shaped the same.

"It made my day, watching him smile with the three of you. Like his little, meaningless life was complete bringing his love to meet his mommy." I squirm in my restraints, while the vile feelings of disgust swarm over me as he brings his face in front of mine.

When his lips touch the tape for a quick kiss, my legs jerk to try and kick him in the balls. How the fuck did he find me? My mind flashes to Mal and Harris. I pray like crazy he left them alone and that I'm the only one he's choosing to torture.

"I knew seeing his smile that day would make this moment here so much more meaningful." He slides his hand between my breasts then begins to grope me again. I hold back a gag while the vomit crawls up my throat. God, I want to kill this motherfucker. My hatred for him was elevated before he ever made the mistake of taking me from my bed. The pain he inflicted on Kaleb was the only strike he needed for me to hate him.

If he gives me one single chance, I'm snapping his fucking neck. I know his filthy hands are violating me, but I have comfort in knowing he can't rape me in this position. He'd have to untie me, and that is something I look forward to him trying.

He may know who I am, but this man doesn't know me at all. I may be being fondled by this monster, but the love I have for myself, my family, and Kaleb will give me the strength to get through this.

He takes both of his hands to the neck of my shirt and rips it down the middle. His face is filled with anticipation as he stands over me, allowing his eyes to scrape over my body. His dark gaze stays glued to the swells of my breast. I can feel my insides twisting with the urge to kill him.

He moves behind me, disappearing from my sight, so I begin to memorize everything in my view. I can hear him pick up something from a table while I'm looking at a blank, white wall in front of me. The carpet looks like that of an older hotel maybe, the ceiling painted with the rough, splattered texture.

He steps back into my view, and with a repulsive grin on his face, he starts twirling a skinning knife with a gut hook in front of me. "I could take these tits off and send them to him. I'm positive that would make the statement I'm not fucking playing around." I don't make a sound. In fact, I'm sure he thinks I'm challenging him with the look in my eyes.

He slides the knife down my cleavage, sending a burning to the surface and the feel of blood dripping on my stomach. The coldness of the knife touches me, while he slides the hook under the thin, lacy material between my breasts, and with a small tug, my bra falls open, freeing and exposing them to his fucked-up torture.

"Nice. Tell me. Does my brother spend time cherishing these?" I keep my head up and look him straight in the eyes, while his rough hands move over my chest and around each of my nipples. "I think I should send him a picture of this. Give him something to remember you by." His voice is full of revenge.

He takes out his phone and pulls one of my nipples tight between his fingers before he takes the picture. I watch his every move as he looks down to his phone, his fingers flying, and I can only assume he sent it to Kaleb, because the phone rings before he has the chance to place it back into his pocket. The smile on his face tells me I'm right.

The sound of Kaleb yelling fills the room even though he's not on speaker. I want to scream and tell him I love him, but I don't. I can't give Ty the satisfaction of knowing I'm gutted inside with what may happen. I know Kaleb is dying inside. I know exactly how he feels.

"You like that? I can send you a few more if you don't shut your fucking mouth. This isn't your game, big brother. I'm calling the shots this time." I can feel Kaleb's pain through the sound of his voice. I'm fighting like hell to keep the tears inside. This fucker can do anything he wants to me, but when I get the chance to kill him, I'm doing it for Kaleb. I'm doing it for the shit he's done to him in the past and the hell he put him through in Mexico.

"The next time I send you something, it'll be a video. We can see if she likes it rough. If she enjoys it up her ass. How she likes being fucked by a real man." He lowers his face to mine, allowing me to hear Kaleb clearly.

"Motherfucker. I swear I'm going to kill you slowly if you do anything to her." His voice punctures through my heart. He's desperate, and I know he's dying to get to me. I have peace, knowing I have the tracker device in my leg. I work to flex my legs, checking for any pain around the device, and don't feel anything. Except for the fact I'm stationery in this goddamn chair, unable to draw his pistol or any other weapon to help me get out of this situation. He's a dick, and one wrong move on his part, and my hands will be out of these restraints and his head will be off that smug set of shoulders.

Thank god, he didn't miraculously find that device. I'm not an idiot, if they can make trackers, they can make devices that detect them just as easily.

"Now, now. Just do what you need to do, and I can promise to let you have her when I'm finished. It can be like the old days. You know, when you fucked a girl after I did." Stare at me all you want, buddy. You won't get a rise out me by talking about Kaleb's past.

He starts pacing back and forth in front of me, those crazy eyes drinking my chest in.

He's tormenting Kaleb with his words and bringing to surface more hatred than I've ever felt in my life.

"You want to hear me fuck her? I can definitely deliver, just keep running your mouth." He rips the tape off of my mouth without any warning and grips between my legs, squeezing until he gets a whimper from me.

"Fucking let him know you're alive." He squeezes harder, and I hold in the piercing pain, not letting him win this jab at Kaleb. I fight through the sharpness and simply say, "I'm alive", releasing a slow exhale with my words, hoping he won't hear my agony through my voice.

He grips harder before he rips his hands from his hold on me, pulling my clit as he does. Shit, the burn in my core travels up my stomach. I clench my legs together the best I can, trying to comfort the pain.

"She's a tough one, Kaleb. I'm gonna have fun breaking her." He hits end on the call, and I grit my teeth harder, feeling the fire light up between my legs.

He sits on the edge of the bed beside me. He's ruthless with his grip again, pulling me toward him with his fingers wrapped tightly around my throat. The grip of the legs on the chair catching on the shaggy carpet causes me to gasp when it gives and he pulls backwards.

"Fuck you, you sick bastard. You'll never get away with this. He'll find you, and he will kill you."

I choke and scream my words out. Hell, I have no idea what kind of plans he has for me. If he wants me to shut up, he can tape my mouth back up, or he can shut me up himself.

"Let me show you how sick I am, sweetheart." He yanks the chair hard, my head flopping backwards, and I have no control as he leans the chair back against the bed and puts his disgusting mouth on mine.

He forces his tongue in my mouth, and I contemplate biting it, but hold back, hoping he'll continue with this distraction of his. I need thirty seconds, that's all.

I need to loosen these ropes. He's not paying a damn bit of attention. His fingers are all over my upper body, his tongue is shoved halfway down my throat. I twist and turn and feel them loosen while they dig and cut deeper into my flesh.

"If I hadn't done my research on you... I'd make the mistake of untying you, but I have. Quite an impressive background you have. You know, you really should tell that country of yours not to announce its Ranger graduates with credentials. It kind of ruins your element of surprise in these sort of situations." He kicks me to the ground, and the chair lands on its side with my back next to the bed. I instantly continue to work my wrists free. I have never felt pain like this in my life. It's raw. It's agonizing, and yet, I hold my ground.

The only noises I'm making are my exhales as I try to catch my breath.

I'm almost there. Wait and watch. He paces, checks his phone, and then glances at me one more time. *I'm going to kill you, Ty. Watch me.*

He moves out of sight when his phone rings, and this time, he starts talking in Spanish.

I twist and fight the ropes, but damn it, he knows how to properly restrain someone, and I can't seem to slip my arms past whatever knots he's tied me up in.

Please get here, guys. Please hurry.

I keep expecting Harris to come barreling through the door, because he has to be the closest.

The fact he's not has me scared he's not able to get to me. Something has to be wrong. He has to be safe. He has to be alive, because I can't comprehend it any other way.

CHAPTER NINETEEN

KALEB

I'm going to kill that motherfucker with my bare hands. Hearing her voice has tipped me over the edge, and if we weren't already on the ground in Alabama, I'd be losing my fucking mind even more.

"Steele, stay ready," I yell over my shoulder. "If he's hurt her, I'll want her flown to a hospital immediately." We all rush to the truck that's waiting to take us, and I can't keep my mind from swarming with all the possibilities.

"Pierce, get to the ranch and check on Harris. He still hasn't moved, and he hasn't fucking answered any of my calls. It's not like him. He'd die before he'd let her be taken."

Jumping in the truck with Kase, Jackson, and Vice, I welcome the speed of Jackson's lead foot.

This is a nightmare. My worst fucking nightmare has come true. Even though I fought like hell to keep her safe, he found out she was my one and only weakness.

I wanted to draw him to me; instead, I left her vulnerable and he now has her.

The reality of how horrible this could be hits me when Jackson slams the truck into park. We all rush to grab our guns and move on the ground at an equal speed toward the hotel. We had our route planned before we landed. Pierce ran the briefing on the plane, detailing every aspect of the surrounding area of her location and the ranch. Everyone has a job and mine is to literally not fall the fuck apart, knowing he has her.

"Can we get a room number?" Kase whispers as we get closer.

Pierce comes back with a quick response. "No, it's on that end in that back wing." He's talking to us through the headgear. He's moving to Harris, but we still keep everyone's ears on the line in case we need to move in either direction.

"Fuck. There are three floors. Goddammit. If he hears us coming, he'll kill her to spite me," I speak into my headgear and wish like fuck I had her in my right ear like usual.

"Watch for signs. I'd guess bottom floor, because he probably had to drag her ass in there," Jackson remarks, then crouches as we all survey the hotel, looking for a sign of which room he's in. My eyes target in on the Florida plates in front of the very end room. I take the heat-censored binoculars and confirm before I order them to move, with hand signals and a low voice.

I see two bodies on the floor, one slowly moving, before I take a quick glance to the next room, which shows nothing. A quick scan of the hotel, and I don't see another body in this entire fucking dump. It would be like him to come to a cockroach castle like this. It's a perfect place to hide the screams. I push that thought to the back of my mind, because I have to. If he fucking killed her, I don't know what I'll do. My mind can't grasp that right now; I need to switch into work mode. It's the hardest damn thing I've ever done, trying to talk my mind into thinking this is a job when I know damn well it's anything but. It's personal. This is his way of dishing out a glorified payback.

"He's on the end. Jackson, come with me, you two take the room next to it just in case it's connected." My voice is deep and low; my mind is set on this being personal. My entire life is inside of that room.

We move fast until I crouch at the door, listening for any noise. I quickly signal the other two that he's behind this door before I step back. Jackson takes off his headgear and knocks on the damn door. His ability to think on his feet in situations like this is why he's really known as Action Jackson. Not once has he failed. Shit, please don't make it be now.

I don't give a fuck how we get in, just as long as she's safe. The rest of us move into shooting positions behind a few parked cars, hidden safely for just the right shot. *Move that fucking curtain and you're gone. One shot, brother. Give me one motherfucking shot, so I can end you.*

"Housekeeping," Jackson yells just before he points his pistol at the knob and then kicks the door open. He takes one step back when the door hits the wall, and my heart stops beating as I watch him rush through the door, lowering his gun as he does.

I'm one step behind him, coming face-to-face with Jade on the floor with my brother's lifeless body on top of hers. She has a rope pulled tight around his neck, and she's still using her strength to choke him. My fearless Jade has the look of a raging killer, and my heart sinks at the possibilities of what she's been through. Her hands are covered in blood, and she looks like she's been through hell to see the devil himself.

"You got him, baby girl. Ease up." Jackson moves in, freeing her grip from the ropes and dragging him off of her body. Her shirt is open, her breasts are exposed, bruises already showing through her porcelain skin, and her face is covered with dirt. Her body stiffens as Jackson drags Ty's body across hers.

I can't get to her fast enough, and I'm on the floor with her before I can even see that she's still restrained. Her feet are tied to a chair, and all I need her to do is look at me. She looks so fragile and worn. What the hell did he do to her?

"I'm here. Jade. Look at me." I touch the side of her face, while her eyes stare blankly ahead. Her breathing is frantic, and I'm looking into eyes I've never seen before.

Jackson slices the ropes that are binding her legs to the chair, and she falls into me. Wrapping my arms around her, I pull her into my arms and hold her cold body as close to me as I can get her.

"Shit, Jade. I'm here." I kiss her forehead and neck while she finally starts to wrap her arms around me. "I'm so fucking sorry I let this happen to you." She doesn't respond with words, only a tighter squeeze, and that's all I need to know she's still with me.

"Is he dead?" she finally speaks. Her voice is wobbly. Her eyes are finally coming back into focus.

"Not yet." I turn to Kase, who's standing over Ty's barely-breathing body. He nods to me and holds his pistol aimed at Ty.

She leans back in my lap and ties her shirt closed. "Where did he hurt you?" I place my hands on her bloodied wrists, seeing the marks from the ropes. Examining her body with my hands frantically, I search for any other signs of injury he caused her before I make him pay for this.

"Here." She places her hand over my heart. I have no idea what I've done to deserve her, but I swear on my own life, I will do everything in my power to make her happy.

"He almost killed me in Mexico when he had you. What happened today doesn't compare to that." I get what she's saying. The hurt I've felt today cut deeper than anything he did to me in Mexico. I have to kiss her and breathe her strength in. The scare I just had still echoes through my head as I place kisses against her cheeks and then her lips.

"I love you, Jade."

"I love you, Kaleb. Now, please finish this, so we can get the hell out of here."

She places her hand on my face, turning it in the direction of Ty. His eyes are wide open with a gleam of hatred reflecting back at me.

I swallow hard, knowing what I'm about to do. I lean forward to kiss her once more before I let Jackson take her outside. Her blood on my shirt only solidifies his fate.

Kase and I pick up his useless body and sit him on the chair he had tied Jade to. I see a skinning knife lying at his feet once I step back to look at him, so I slide it toward me, using my boot. Picking it up, I see blood on the blade and realize this is what he cut her with. It's a fucking knife used to gut something. The blade is so sharp it will skin a person alive. I should use his weapon of choice as it's meant to be used.

Kase is working on restraining him, and I begin to battle with what I want to make sure he hears as his last words. I pick up my own pistol off the table behind him. He has many weapons laid out like he planned to have variety when he worked her over. I'm still keeping score.

"I told you not to fucking touch her." I lean over him, making sure it's my eyes he sees. "I told you if you so much as took a breath near her, I'd fucking kill you. Then I get here to find her bloody and roughed up."

"Fuck you." His voice is raspy and rough speaking through the damage Jade caused on his throat. I can only imagine the force she used on him until we got here. The rage on her face told me what I needed to know.

"I told you to leave mom and Amelie alone, but you just couldn't listen. Tell me, Ty... Why the fuck would you get into all the shit you're into? A fucking drug cartel. Terrorist hiding. International sex trade operation. Not to mention providing illegal weapons of mass destruction to criminals all over the world."

I lean forward again, giving him a chance to answer.

"She tasted so fuckin sweet, brother. Next time you put your dick inside that pussy... Just know I've been there." My hand instantly grips his neck in anger, and I squeeze and draw the life out of him with my bare hand, while I watch his eyes stare into mine. He's testing me and trying to get a rise out of me.

"It's an honor to rid the world of your disgusting, vile ass. Say hello to your friends in hell. I'll be sending you a few more every chance I get." He closes his eyes, and for a brief second, he looks like my father did. I grip tighter and twirl the knife in my other hand, waiting for the perfect time to stop. Once he's about to go, I release his throat. "Stay with me, brother.... I have so much more to do to you before you go." I open-palm slap him in the face, and his head snaps back. A loud, guttural sound breaks free from his throat, allowing his deceitful eyes to bolt wide open.

"You call this torture," he taunts. "I call this you being the pussy-ass motherfucker I always knew you were. You could never control me, could you, Kaleb. Not like you did mom. Anything Kaleb wanted, Kaleb got. And Amelie, all you did was

coddle her. Protected her. Turned her into who you wanted
her to be. And then you left them, just like our father, you
fucking left." His voice is so damn raspy, so low, but I hear him.
Every shitty, jealous word.

"So you decide to what? Get even with me by fucking
your life up, by becoming some big drug-dealing scumbag who
betrays his family, his country, and our mom out of jealousy? Is
that what you're saying? You're blaming me because I did right
by my life, by my country. You're so fucking warped and way
off base. I fucking loved you," I roar. "I drug you home after
you had your ass beat. I paid your debts to keep those measly
go-betweens from killing you. I tried to get you help. So don't
blame me for the fucked-up life you created for yourself. You're
delusional if you think I'll buy into any of this. You fucking
promised me when I left that you would stay clean. That your
last stint in rehab made you realize you wanted more out of
your life. You fucked up, not me. Not our father. YOU." I flip
the knife around in my hand. I've got a woman waiting for
me. I've got a mother who I'm going to have to tell that her son
really is dead. I've got time, which is a hell of a lot more than he
does.

"You remember this when your soul and your mind are
being tortured for eternity in hell, brother. Remember that I'm
the one who sent you there. But you're the one who put

yourself there. I could've dealt with the shit you've done to me, but I'll never let you live after you've threatened Jade. Take these words to hell with you." He squirms in Kase's arms when he sees the knife lodged against the center of his chest. I hesitate, only to make sure I look him in the eyes as I plunge it into his flesh and twist and gut the hell out of him. He sputters as his warm blood drips all over my hand. I turn, rotate, and drag the knife down the center of his chest. I watch the blood trickle out of the corners of his mouth and his eyes begin to glass over. *I just killed my brother.*

"Get the hell out of here, man. Let me finish this." Kase looks at me like a true brother would. One who defends and honors the other. One who has your back. One who helps you clean up your mess. One who loves you.

I clean the blood off my hands, using the sink in the bathroom. The rusty water mixed with the bright-red blood turns a hazy, deep orange. I've killed him. It's over. No more wondering what the hell he's doing, where he is, or if he's even breathing. I've worried about him for years. Ty was unreachable. He was too far gone.

He was never my brother, not like the men who are all standing outside. Jackson is standing with his arm around my woman, protecting and comforting her. No. Blood doesn't mean family. Loyalty makes a brother.

"You good, baby?" I ask Jade when I reach her, bringing her into my arms, where she belongs.

"Yes. Are you?" I nod. There's nothing left to be said about what happened in that room. Not here, not ever again. I'll figure out how to tell my mom and sister he's gone, but right now, I need to get her checked out and find out about Harris and Mallory.

"Anyone hear from Pierce?" I place my arm around her shoulders and guide her to the passenger side of the truck.

"They've taken Harris to the hospital. He was shot in the shoulder," Jackson tells me. No humor in his words. No joking.

"Is he alright? Coherent? What about Mallory?" I climb into the truck, grab a hold of Jade by her waist, and pull her onto my lap. No damn way is she sitting in the back cab. I need her as close to me as fucking possible.

"He'll be fine. Mallory's shaken up quite a bit." Thank god. If anything had happened to either one of them, that nightmare would have haunted me for the rest of my life.

"We need to get you checked out too. I'll take care of calling your superior." I place my hand on her head while her body relaxes into mine.

"Thank you, "she whispers. She's changed me. This woman whose photo ran across my desk months ago has single-handedly changed me.

She's softened me. Whether I want to believe it or not, she has. My life is much more complicated with another person to worry about, but I wouldn't change it for the world.

"I love you." I have to say it to her again. I have to smell her hair and feel her skin. The chaos of my mind since I left her bed proves to me I'm much better with her than I am away from her.

CHAPTER TWENTY

KALEB

I hold Jade until we get to the hospital. She allows me to caress her back and whisper into her ear, but I can feel that she's distant. I'm fighting to figure out if it's the psyche of being kidnapped and tortured, or if it's about us.

"Tell me he didn't rape you." I guide her face to meet mine. I need to see her reactions to everything I ask.

"No, he didn't."

"Tell me what he did." I try not to hate a man whom I've already made pay for his torture for her, but I can't. I look down at a cut down her cleavage and feel my anger boil even higher.

"Kaleb, I'm not reliving that again. I'm fine. He's not a threat anymore, and we made it out alive."

"Tell me what you're thinking then." She won't look at me now and chooses to lay her head back against my chest.

"Nothing. I just need to see that Harris and Mal are ok." I can give her that. I feel the same way.

"We'll get you checked out and I'll have the guys update us on them. I promise we'll do what we can to make sure they have the best medical treatment possible if they need anything." I try to make her feel better, all the while hoping I'll feel some relief myself.

"Some things can't be fixed like that, Kaleb. It's not the surface scars I'm worried about." Her words hit home for me. The internal hurt is far worse than any damage done to the surface.

"I know." I can't say anything different about that. I do know. I can't make her feel any better, knowing she's probably right. I just pray to god my brother didn't do anything detrimental to either of them. Caressing her back calms me. I feel close to her even though I can feel her pulling away.

We pull into the hospital drive, where medical personnel meet us outside. Jackson is instantly asking about Harris and Mallory, while I'm guiding Jade out of the truck. She refuses a wheelchair like the stubborn woman she is, and we walk inside to a small room to wait for a doctor.

She won't look at me, and it's getting to me. I shouldn't be making this about me, but it is about us. I'd give anything for just one normal fucking day with her.

"Jade, why do I feel like you're checking out on me?"

"Kaleb. We can talk once I know Harris and Mallory are ok. Until then, I'm still in my own war zone on a mission." She scoots onto the hospital bed, and I step outside in hopes of seeing some sign of the others. Jackson is walking down the hall toward me, so I watch for any signs he has bad news. He seems to be indifferent.

"Mallory is upset and Harris is in surgery. I asked them to get Jade and Mallory in the same room as soon as possible. They're going to move Jade here in a few minutes."

"What's the prognosis of Harris' injuries?"

"Shoulder is all I've heard. Should be out of surgery in a few hours." A few hours will feel like an eternity with Jade and Mallory together while we wait for his news, but I'll be there for both of them.

Jade is standing in the doorway with me just as the doctor comes in. "Alright, Ms. Elliott, let's see your injuries." She steps back into the room and unties her shirt as I close the door. The jagged cut down her torso isn't too deep, but any blood shed from her body is too much in my opinion. I'm just glad she won't require stitches.

"Were you sexually assaulted?" His cold question heats me up with rage. I'm so damn thankful her answer is no, because I can't even imagine the guilt I'd feel if it were yes.

"No. He just cut me here, I have rope burns from the restraints, and he pulled my hair." She points to her chest and then looks over at me. "Other than that, it was just threats and a forceful kiss." *He fucking kissed her.* I work hard to hide my fury, but I know I'm not succeeding. Remember, Kaleb, he's dead. He can't hurt her ever again.

"Alright, we'll get this cleaned up. You won't be needing stitches on this. You're a very lucky woman. I've seen some terrible cases come through here. When I heard we had a kidnapping victim headed our way, I was worried what I'd see today."

"Thank you, doctor. Can I see my friend Mallory? I need to see what he did to her."

"Sure thing. Let me just say, we're very lucky today on both cases. Let us get you cleaned up, but why don't I keep you overnight for observation. That'll give you a room in to stay next to your friend. I told her I'd keep her in here until the guy she came in with was released. I shouldn't share anything with you legally, but I want you to know he's going to be just fine. The bullet is being removed now, and it looks like he'll have full use of his shoulder if everything goes as planned during surgery." We both welcome the information, knowing he wasn't supposed to share anything. I can imagine he's trying to calm Jade and bring some peace to her torn-up demeanor.

"Thank you, doctor. I needed that information."

"Absolutely. Now, be patient for me and we'll get you taken care of." Patience is something neither of us is good at but lately we've been forced into. I look at Jade and wonder if I'm more impatient about what she's not saying, or if I need to see the other two are good with my own two eyes.

"Please, stop looking at me like I'm killing you slowly."

"Are you sure you're not?"

"Kaleb. I can't do this shit. I can't feel like I'm dying inside because you're in danger. I can't feel like I'm inferior because you shut me out." I hear that last sentence, and my heart drops. I've done this to her. In all my focus of protecting her, I never once considered what it would look like on her end of it. I wanted her safe. Period.

I move to her instantly and stop just in front of her. She's sitting on the bed with her shirt still open, but she's covered. I struggle for the right words, knowing I have to do this right. I have to make her understand that everything I did was because of my love for her.

"Jade. I'm sorry if I made you feel inferior, but that is in no way how I feel. In fact, to me, you're so far above my level of importance I can't even consider the thought of losing you. It terrifies me that you expose me the way you do. You leave me open and raw with just one frown on your face. I love you with my entire being, and I can't comprehend my life without you. Please, don't entertain any thoughts of trying to leave me, because I can't live with that."

"Kaleb, I can't live like this. The way you treated me the past few days is unacceptable, and you know me better than that. I've worked my ass off to be treated with the respect I deserve. If I can't get that from the man I love, then how do I expect my fellow soldiers to give it to me?" I want to pull her against my chest and hold her against me. If I could just communicate with my body, I know she'd understand me, but I know this isn't the time or the place.

"I'm sorry. I do respect you more than you'll ever know. In fact, I'd step into hell if it meant you'd be safe."

"I know you would. I'm not doubting your desire to protect me. I'm doubting your ability to differentiate when you're protecting me and when you're simply shutting me out because you don't want me on a mission that *might* go wrong. They could all go wrong, Kaleb." She stands on the step at the end of the bed, allowing our faces to be even closer. Looking straight into my eyes, she continues. "I doubt my own ability to be calm when you're away for work. I don't know how you'll react when I'm gone on my own missions. How will we ever deal with the chaos that surrounds our jobs?" I can't suggest what I want to. I'd never ask her to change her career for me, but I wish like hell I could have her next to me every day of my life.

"We'll learn to adjust, because there's no other fucking option, Jade."

EPILOGUE
THREE MONTHS LATER
Kaleb

"Get your sexy ass out here." I pound on the bathroom door in the villa we rented for two weeks in Bali.

It's been a long three months to get here. Paperwork up the ass when we flew back to Florida after a brief hospital stay with Mallory. Jade's scars on her wrist are finally healed.

Harris is still off of active duty while he pisses and moans every damn day about the rigorous physical therapy he has to go through. I can imagine how fucking bored and eager he is to get back out on missions. I understand completely where he's coming from. I'd be out of my mind too if all I did was shuffle papers around on a desk all day long.

The man I hated when we first met has become one of my best friends. One of my closest brothers. He'd proven himself before the night I took my brother's life, but taking a bullet for Jade in the middle of the night when he saw a shadow slither by his room put him at the top of my list.

I know he feels guilty for not being able to stop him from taking her. No matter how hard I've tried to convince him it wasn't his fault, he still carries that burden on his shoulders. I can't help him with that. We all have our guilt we're trying to deal with. He has to work that shit out on his own. He's a damn good man. One I look forward to having by my side in the future. One I will gladly give my life for.

"Don't rush me. I have to be perfect." Jade and her smart-ass mouth hollers back at me through the wooden door. I'm about ready to bust the fucking door down and tag her ass right on the bathroom counter if she doesn't hurry the fuck up.

"I'll be by the pool. You have five minutes."

"What the hell ever, Kaleb. Don't be so damn bossy." *Fuck.* I love her. Our life will never be boring. Not with the way we both still fight each other for control. I may pretend at times, but she knows damn well who's in charge here. She controls my heart, which I learned very quickly, controls me.

Moving away from the door, I snag my phone off the kitchen counter and make my way outside, knowing good and well she's going to be longer than five minutes. Whatever the fuck surprise she has for me sure as hell can't compare to the one I have for her. I start to remember our talk at the hospital. All I wanted to do was take her home and hold her in my arms, so I could pretend we didn't need to have a talk. *The talk* I'm willing to admit scared the shit out of me.

I remember every damn word she said and I remember every single promise I made to her. Treating her like my equal is all I'll ever do. She agreed to be with me as long as we don't keep any secrets. I know this will be difficult as missions come, but I know we'll work through it all in time.

Now, here I stand, staring into the light blue sky, the sun blazing down over the clear ocean water in its numerous shades of blues and turquoise. This is fucking paradise. Never in a million years would I think

I'd be standing here, waiting for a woman to grace me with her presence so we could swim in the ocean or lie by the pool. Or fuck like we've been doing for the past few days. Christ, I'll never get tired of having her wrapped around my cock.

I need to quit thinking about her for one minute and call my mom. It's her birthday.

Powering up my phone, I find her name and hit call. This woman is the epitome of strength and courage if ever there was one. The minute we pulled into the hospital parking lot, Jackson pulled out his phone and called Vice and Ace. Told them it was over and to get on a plane and fly my mom and sister to me.

By the time they reached us, Jade was ready to go. Harris was out of surgery already, while Mallory stayed by his side. Mallory is another contradiction I need to figure out. Something's up with her. Whenever I bring it up to Jade, she says Mallory is still fighting her demons over what happened that night. I'm not sure what to think about it all.

"Hey, son," my mom answers, and her still delicate voice softens me every time I talk to her. I lied to her face about what happened. I told her Ty was dead when we found him, killed by one of his drug lords, guessing it was over the money he owed them for drugs. I couldn't hide the fact that Jade was in the hospital, but I lied about that too. Both Jade and I did. We told her the same drug lord he owed money had taken Jade and brought her to the motel, hoping I would pay his debt. Then I was too late to save him. Jade had told them there was no way I'd help out. They tied her up and roughed her up because she wouldn't call me.

The look in my mom's eyes when she finally realized her son was truly dead is a look I will never forget. A piece of her died that day. A piece she'll struggle with for the rest of her life. The sad part about it all is, I tried to sugarcoat it the best I could, but there was no way I could come up with an easy way to tell her. I sure as hell wasn't going to tell her the truth. I know my mom though. She knows I didn't tell her everything. She knows I killed him, but she'll never tell me she does. She'll take it to her grave to save me the pain and suffering she knows I struggle with every day and will for the rest of my life. I killed my brother.

"Happy Birthday, old lady." I chuckle.

"Thank you, Kaleb. You two having fun?" Her idea of fun and mine are two different things.

"Fuck, yes, we are."

"Language, boy," she reprimands me, and I laugh some more.

"Yes, ma'am."

"I appreciate the call, Kaleb. Now, go. Enjoy yourself. Lord knows you two have earned it." I sigh heavily, knowing she's still dealing with the aftermath of all of this, while I'm here trying to forget and moving forward with Jade, hoping to start a beginning to our normal sooner rather than later.

"I love you, mom." I close my eyes. Her 'I love you' back to me becomes lodged in my throat.

I hang up the phone and toss it on the lounge chair before I spin around, ready to start bitching about whatever the hell is taking her so long, but instead, my mouth hits the floor. She's standing there, naked. Her nipples harden when I look at them. Her body glows. Her eyes turn dark, and that sweet spot between her legs has my cock hard.

"Is this my surprise? Because if you think for one second you're going swimming like that, you've lost your fucking mind." I may have softened up a little bit after the hell we've been through, but there is no damn way she's walking out with her sinful body showing like that. Hell, that'll have every man's head turning, doing a double take to get another look at her when we walk by them.

"I'm lying out naked. And no, this isn't your surprise." She moves in my direction. I stop her by blocking her with my body before she crosses over the threshold of the open breezeway that leads to the pool and the beach.

My itching fingers grip her ass, pulling her flush against my cock. Her brows quirk up.

"I'll decide if you get to take another step out of here like that or not. Now, tell me what this big surprise is about."

"I'm retiring from the Army when my term is up in two months." I look down at her to search for any sign she feels regret over her decision. Her giant smile and playful attitude tell me she's relieved this is coming. I can't say I'm not fucking thrilled, because I am. I want nothing more than to have her by my side every single day and night.

"You sure this is what you want?" I have to give her the opportunity to change her mind here. This has been her entire life for years now. I know how hard this decision was for me.

"I'm positive. Kaleb, I'll still be able to do what I've trained my whole career for, but now I'll be able to do it all with you." She moves her fingers over my ass and squeezes with both hands. "Plus, you need someone to save your gorgeous ass out there." Her teasing only makes this much sweeter.

"How did I get so lucky?" My internal thoughts escape my mouth before I have the chance to hold them in. She smiles through her kiss when I pull her legs up around my waist. "Guess it was fate... Or some of that romantic crap people talk about." Her laughter sends a jolt straight through me. I take a moment to think about where I am in my life. I'm in love with the woman of my dreams. This is exactly what I hoped I'd get with Jade. It's exactly what I prayed for in the desert, and it's what I've always wanted to feel before I met her. She's it for me. She has my heart, my mind, and my fucking soul.

"Jade Elliott, future Mrs. Maverick... You're not fucking leaving this room without some damn clothes on. You'll either cover yourself with some little piece of material you own, or I'll cover you with my body. You'll have sunburnt feet, because you'll have them wrapped around my ass while I fuck you all damn day."

"You're so damn bossy." She wraps her arms around my neck and pulls her face close to mine. Nose to nose, she's looking into my eyes.

"Are you just now figuring that out?"

"No, I vaguely remember thinking it the first time I met you." She pulls another smile from me, and I start walking us back to the bedroom. This place is gorgeous, and I love the open feel of the beach right into the bedroom. It doesn't help knowing that if anyone walks by, they'll be able to hear us fucking. I don't mind that one bit, but they won't be able to see. Our villa is on stilts, sitting high enough that we have the privacy we came here to have.

"Come with me tomorrow." I've been trying to decide how to do this. We're not a normal couple. It's only fitting that this be different as well.

"Where?" She looks into my eyes after I lay her on her back on the bed. I crawl over her body and prepare for this next chapter in my life. One I'm dying to get started on.

"I want a new tattoo." She smiles, knowing I've been itching for a new one.

"What are you thinking about getting?" She kisses my lips as I lower myself playfully on her body.

"I'm thinking a ring or something. Maybe your name across my ass." Her laugher fills the room, and I take this opportunity to kiss the crook of her neck, gliding my body in place on top of hers.

"I do own it."

I sit up and look straight into her eyes again. Yes, she does own it. She owns me and my future. If she's not involved in it, I want nothing to do with it.

"You do. Now, let's make it official. Marry me, Jade." She pulls her smile into a serious facial expression, looking for any sign I'm kidding here. She won't find one. I'm dead serious. I want her in my life forever.

"Jade. You're my forever. With or without a shiny fucking ring, you're mine and I'm yours. I don't want some bullshit piece of gold to wear to commit my love to you. I want it permanently on my body to last forever. Just like we will." She starts to slowly smile while she continues to study my face.

She pulls me down into a passionate kiss before she says the words I hoped she'd say.

"Yes, Sir." Fuck. That's it. I'm done forever.

If you'd like to receive text notifications for our next release, please text 'FIRE' to 213-802-5257!

Coming this Summer in the Elite Forces Series... Harris' story!

Acknowledgements by Hilary

I read my acknowledgements from ICE and can't think of one single word I'd change for this book! It was the same crew bringing it together for this one and the same amazing people supporting us. So please don't get mad at me, but I feel I said it best in ICE! So here are my acknowledgements!

Kathy Coopmans is an amazing woman and it has been an absolute pleasure beginning this journey with her. I know this series will be epic because every single time we talk…. We enhance it. The story unfolded beautifully as we both allowed the creative words to flow. The lineup we have in mind is going to blow people away and I can't wait to stand proud as fuck right next to you! (Yes I'm the one that says fuck mostly through the book if you haven't guessed lol.)

My husband and kids are my life. Without their love and support I could never do any of this. It is through them that I have learned to love, live, and take chances. My heart is full because of these four.

Golden… My furious man! You have been amazing to work with over the past two years! This series will provide new ventures for us both and I know we'll stand stronger for it in the end! Lots of love my friend!

Dylan and Tessi. My two fav hotties right now! How in the world do you two plan to deal with us? You're stuck with us on this journey and I couldn't be prouder! Everything happens for a reason and I know deep in my heart this collaboration is just the beginning of careers that will flourish! It's through the love and support as a team that we will all conquer great things!

Julia- You made us look good in this! Thanks for your cooperation in making this happen! We're so please to have you on board!

Betas... I want to thank you all for pointing out the imperfections! We loved hearing from each of you and appreciate you taking the time to help make this possible!

SE Hall and Victoria Ashley- My loves! I'm so glad you love Kaleb! We can maybe work out some sort of trade with your guys if you really think you're going to claim him! He's a hot one so bring your best to the table! I know you both have them!

Our loyal followers who will love this and share it like crazy, just like they always do. It is because of you that we keep writing with the urgency we do. We can't wait to share our stories with you so we can see how you react. Thank you for always allowing us to be a part of your lives through our words.

Read more of Hilary's Books

Six (Blade and Tori's story)

Seven (Coming Soon)

Rebel Walking Series

      In A Heartbeat

      Heaven Sent

      Banded Together

      No Strings Attached

      Hold Me Closer

      Fighting the Odds

      Never Say Goodbye

      Whiskey Dreams

Inked Brothers Series

      Jake One

      Jake Two

Bryant Brothers Series

      Don't Close Your Eyes

Acknowledgements by Kathy

This part is easy for me. I have to thank my partner Hilary Storm for this unbelievable journey we are on.

We are having the time our lives writing together. Even though we write differently, we still fit together perfectly. The way we consume each other's ideas. Focus and plan. Our phone calls, text messages, all of it has been done in a way no words can express. The greatest thing about this is, our friendship has blossomed into one of a sisterhood. I will cherish her forever.

To my husband and children- Day in you hear about my stories. The support, the pride you show me when you honest to god listen will last beyond this lifetime.

To our editor Julia Goda- Snap woman. You are as badass as they come.

To Golden Czermak- The photo god. The genius. Thank you for everything you have done to make this possible for the two of us.

To our cover models Tessi and Dylan- We both look forward to this wild and crazy ride the four of us are about to set sail on. Damn, this is going to be fun.

To our BETA readers- We nailed it you said. Here's to all of you.

To Helena Rizzuto- My friend, my sanity. What can I say, except thank you for always having my back. For jumping on board with this project and running free like the wind to help Hilary and I succeed.

To Lisa Shilling Heinz of The Rock Stars of Romance- You never disappoint me. You are one hell of a business woman. I appreciate you more than you will ever know.

To every reader/ blogger/ author who has shared. Will read. Leave an honest review for ICE. Hilary nor I could do any of this without you. Our work would lay stagnant on our computers. We would have nothing. It's because of you we do. I'm eternally grateful.

To Victoria Ashley and SE Hall. Both Hilary and I are very sorry to tell you that Kaleb Maverick is ours. Although we may share. Maybe!

Kathy's books

The Shelter Me Series

Shelter Me

Rescue Me

Keep Me

The Contrite Duet

Contrite

Reprisal

The Syndicate Series

The Wrath of Cain

The Redemption of Roan

The Absolution of Aidan

The Deliverance of Dilan

Made in the USA
San Bernardino, CA
04 June 2016